CURVE BALLS & SECOND CHANCES

PICKWICK PIRATE QUEENS SOFTBALL ROMANCE SERIES
BOOK ONE

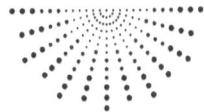

SUSAN BOLES

Copyright 2025 by Susan Boles

ISBN 978-09993868-5-9

"Sometimes, a new beginning looks an awful lot like a second chance."

CHAPTER ONE

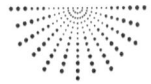

hwack!

The red-stitched neon yellow ball lifted off the edge of the bat and sailed straight toward the blazing sun.

Metal bleachers screeched a protest as Rose McAllister watched the play, then stood up, ball cap tugged low over sunglasses to counter the blinding afternoon light. Cupping her hands around her mouth, she shouted across the field.

"Ginny! You gotta *watch* the ball, hun. That sun's not gonna catch it for you!"

Out in right field, Ginny half-turned, glove poised, head tilted upward.

The ball landed about five feet behind her, rolling to the fence where Allie, playing backup, scooped it clean and zipped it toward second.

The dugout erupted in a chorus of "Oooohs!"—half good-natured ribbing, half actual coaching critique.

Rose kept her game face on. Her players knew better than to mistake her humor for leniency. A few had even learned that lesson the hard way. Usually after a few laps around the bases

But you didn't run the best women's slow-pitch softball team in Hardin County by being soft. And she was determined to win the regional competition this year. A little push now might be the magic ingredient to make that happen. Last year had been so close she'd been almost physically ill when they'd lost by one run in the end.

She still couldn't hear the words "pop fly" without wanting to throw something.

"Okay, hustle up!" Rose called. "Back to positions. Let's run it again!"

Bats clinked as players swapped spots. Dani jogged to shortstop, flipping her glove in the air and catching it without looking. Maggie ambled toward third with all the enthusiasm of someone heading for a dental appointment.

"Move it, Mags!" Rose barked.

Maggie shot her a look over her shoulder. "You can't rush art, Coach."

Rose smirked despite herself. "It's not art if it ends up in the dirt."

On the next hit, Allie cracked a low liner that zipped right past second base. Dani dove for it, glove outstretched and managed to stop the ball from getting to the outfield, though she landed in a cloud of dust big enough to make the first baseman cough.

"That's what I'm talkin' about!" Rose shouted. "Nice stop, Dani!"

"Okay! Let's switch up players. I want everyone running all the drills."

Ginny, the team's youngest player, jogged off the field with a sheepish grin, stopping at the foot of the bleachers. "Sorry, Coach."

"Don't *tell* me," Rose said, tossing her an ice-cold bottle of water from the cooler at her feet. "Just *show* me you can keep your glove outta your hair next time."

As Ginny nodded, cracked the bottle of water and trotted to the dugout, Rose turned back toward the field, shielding her eyes from the sun. Even the hat and sunglasses weren't cutting the glare. This late in the afternoon the angle was near impossible to defeat. Add in the breathless quality of the air and it was a recipe for sweat and short tempers.

The June heat lay over the field like a thick, wet blanket—humid, unrelenting, and familiar in the way only a Southern summer could be. Somewhere beyond the outfield fence, cicadas droned their summer chorus, and a whiff of fresh-cut grass mixed with the dusty scent of the infield.

"Alright, ladies!" Rose called, clapping her hands. "Let's run it again—outfielders, talk to each other out there! If you lose it in the sun, call it so the next gal can take over!"

The next batter stepped up, kicking a little red dirt over the white chalk line of the batter's box. Rose watched her settle in, the faint tang of leather and dust in the air. The cicadas had restarted their droning chorus in the trees beyond the fence, blending with the distant hum of boat engines from the lake a half-mile away.

Crack! The ball soared toward deep left.

"Yours, Amber!" someone hollered. Amber charged forward, snagged it mid-bounce, and rifled it to second in one smooth motion.

"Nice hustle!" Rose shouted. She wiped sweat from the back of her neck with a small towel, then perched on the top bleacher rail for a better view.

Bats cracked, gloves popped, and a few muttered curses drifted across the diamond as the infield ran a double-play drill.

This field, these women, this *team*—they were hers. Steady. Dependable. The things she'd come to rely on as must haves in her life. And she'd built it from scratch over time.

Unlike a certain man whose name she hadn't said out loud in years. The one who'd arrived back in town so unexpectedly last month sending her heart into cartwheels and her stomach dropping to her feet. All that and she hadn't laid eyes on him yet. The past had come home. And she wasn't sure she was ready for it.

And then, just as the next pitch floated toward home plate, a voice—low, sure, painfully familiar—cut across the summer air.

"Rose."

The tiny hairs at the base of her neck stood up in response.

She turned.

Speak of the devil. Had her thoughts conjured him up? Even knowing he was back in town and that this meeting was inevitable hadn't softened the shock.

Acen Wheeler stood at the edge of the dugout, arms crossed over his chest, ball cap tugged low. His dark hair shorter now, just barely showing along the edges of a ball cap advertising the team he'd played pro for -- and peppered with gray at the temples. The years had filled him out, broader shoulders, a deeper jawline softened a bit by a close-cut beard—but his eyes were the same sharp, smoky blue. The same eyes she'd once memorized every shade of, right before he broke her heart.

For a second, she couldn't speak. Couldn't breathe. Time swirled backward as she drowned in that gaze.

A door slammed shut long ago creaked open and the betrayal sprang forward like a hungry cat just waiting for an opportunity to remind her. Rounding the corner of the building on graduation night. Excitement fizzing in her blood like champagne. The future a long, shining, endless road in front of her.

Her brain had taken a minute to compute what

her eyes were telling her. When eyes and brain came to an agreement, Rose swallowed back a sob. In the shadow of the building, Acen and her friend Briana stood in a tight embrace. Bodies touching chest to feet and lips locked together. She'd fled with her tattered dreams scattered on the hard asphalt behind her.

Acen had left for college the next day.

Briana not long after.

And she'd stayed behind in Pickwick Bend.

Until today she hadn't seen or spoken to Acen in twenty years. Twenty long hard years of building a life totally different from the one she'd imagined before that fateful graduation night.

Then muscle memory kicked in. Never let them see you sweat. She couldn't remember who'd said that, but it would become her mantra around this man.

"Well, I'll be damned," she said, folding her arms and tilting her chin, grateful that her own eyes were hidden by the dark sunglasses she wore. Oh, so casual. That's how to play this moment. But her heart fluttered against her ribs. Good thing no one could see that. "Thought I smelled regret."

His mouth tugged into a half-smile. "Still got that fire, huh?"

She eased down the bleacher steps and moved closer, just enough for her team to pretend they weren't eavesdropping from behind the fence. Even though she could almost feel the wind generated from so many sets of ears flapping to catch every word. "What are you doing here?"

"Riley didn't tell you?" Acen asked, eyebrows raised.

"Riley tells me plenty. Doesn't mean I listen." She hoped the lie didn't sound as loud to everyone listening as it did to her. She'd known. Her twin brother would never have let her come face-to-face with Acen unprepared.

"I'm back," he said simply, and somehow that felt like a threat and a confession all at once.

"Back for how long?"

"Indefinitely. I'm moving in with my dad for a bit. Helping out with some things. He's getting older and it's harder for him to handle everything these days."

She nodded as she studied him, heart tight in her chest. He looked older. Tired. Still… *dangerous* in the way that only a first love could be.

"Well," she said finally, stepping around him toward her equipment bag lying on the bench behind him. "Welcome back." She pointed over her shoulder. "The parking lot's that way."

He didn't leave. Of course he didn't. When had anything ever come easy for her?

"You still coaching?" he asked, gesturing to the field.

"Looks like it."

"You were always good at bossing people around."

Rose zipped her bag slowly, deliberately. "And you were always good at pretending you liked being told what to do."

That half-smile again. She hated how it twisted in her chest.

Before she could say something she'd regret—or something she'd want to repeat—her best friend Tasha came jogging over, glancing between them. Her eyes full of concern.

"You okay, Rose?" she asked, suspiciously chipper.

"Peachy," Rose said. "We're just being polite. And Acen was just leaving."

Acen gave Tasha a nod. "Good to see you, Tash."

"You too," she said carefully. Then, to Rose: "Want me to bring the bats to your truck?"

Rose threw Acen one last glance. "That would be great."

"That's a wrap, ladies!" She said to the group crowded into the dugout. "Great practice. Get some rest. You're gonna to need it." A chorus of groans met that statement.

As she and Tasha walked away, summer scorched grass crackling beneath their feet, Tasha whispered under her breath, "*Wow.* Time has been good to Acen Wheeler for sure."

"Unfortunately," Rose muttered, hoping Tasha would drop the subject.

"Girl. If he were any hotter, I'd need a permit to look at him in public."

Rose didn't smile. Not even a little. Instead, she threw her bag into the back of the beat-up pickup she'd gotten for a steal of a deal at an auction years ago and had put over a hundred thousand miles on over the years.

"Catch you later at the coffee shop," she said to Tasha. "I'll be open late tonight for the tourist season. Cindy is probably ready to head home by now." She'd hired Cindy to take care of the coffee shop when she needed to be at practice and games during the summer. It worked well for both of them. Cindy got to earn some extra money and mingle with the public and Rose got to be with her beloved ball team.

She ran her hand slowly along the scuffed blue paint of the door of the truck. *The same color as Acen's eyes.* Whispered her brain. Good grief. Please don't let everything start reminding her of him. That was a distraction she did not need in her life with the regional playoff games about to start.

In their one conversation about the man, Riley had told her Acen had never married. Not that she cared. But it threw her off balance in a way that she didn't like. And that today her heart had responded so easily to him after all the silence. Especially since their relationship had ended with no explanation.

She'd tried to get something out of Briana back then. Back when Briana still deigned to come home for a family visit once a year. But Briana had been silent as the tomb. Defensive and edgy. Understandable since she'd more or less stolen Rose's longtime boyfriend.

And, just like that, their long-standing friendship

had vanished. Along with Briana herself. She'd stopped visiting after a few years.

Had Acen and Briana been together in those years of silence? A big part of her didn't want to know. *Liar,* whispered her brain. She desperately wanted to understand what had happened all those years ago. Just so she could finally put it all to bed in her head. *Sure, that's why"* her traitor brain chimed in.

She climbed into the driver's seat and slammed the door--- hard. To shut up her brain and its smart remarks.

CHAPTER TWO

Acen leaned against the porch railing, sipping sweet tea from a sweating mason jar and wishing it was a beer. After the meeting with Rose earlier he sure could use one. Instead, he took another sip of tea and turned his eyes upward. The sky had changed to that deep Tennessee indigo, and cicadas buzzed like they'd been waiting twenty years just to welcome him back. A warm breeze drifted through the yard, carrying the faint scent of honeysuckle and freshly cut grass. Somewhere down the road, a dog barked twice, then gave up, deciding it was too hot for the trouble.

The Wheeler house hadn't changed much over the years that he'd been gone.

The shutters still hung just a bit crooked on the upstairs windows. His dad had tried to get the boys to climb up and fix them years ago, but somehow, there had always been something more interesting to do. Somewhere else they urgently needed to be.

The porch still sagged just a little in the middle, another project they'd never gotten around to fixing, but the joists underneath still held firm. A testament to old-time builders and quality foundations. And there was still that old moss green metal glider swing with a little rust on the corners and creases due to exposure to the elements—the one he and his best friend Riley used to sit on when summer nights stretched long and full of stories and the future seemed bright and shining to the young men they'd been on the verge of becoming.

And with Rose, too. Young love, laughter, stolen kisses. The brush of her hair against his cheek when she leaned in, the way she'd laugh into his neck before darting away. He shrugged the memories away, forcing himself back to the present.

"You talk to her yet?" Riley asked, stepping out onto the porch with his own mason jar of tea in hand. At the Wheeler house everyone was family who served themselves from the bottomless pitcher of sweet tea that was a mainstay in the Wheeler refrigerator.

Acen didn't answer right away. Still caught up a bit in memories of the past. And things that once done could never be undone.

"I take it from your silence that she didn't throw herself into your arms."

Acen snorted, pushed away from the porch railing.

"She didn't throw anything. That was almost more concerning."

Riley lowered himself into the glider and absently picked at a rusty spot on the arm, eyes on his old friend. "You didn't expect her to still be mad?"

"I just..." Acen paused, swirling the tea in his glass, leaned against the railing again. "I don't know. It's been twenty years."

"Yeah, and you ghosted her for all twenty." Riley kicked long legs clad in faded jeans out in front of him, slouched to a more comfortable position. "I never asked you about it because I didn't want to put you on the spot or strain our friendship. I figured whatever happened was between you and Rose. And it was up to the two of you to work it out. But now you're back in town, it's going to be hard."

Acen winced. "I didn't ghost her." But in his heart, he knew he had. And the reckoning was at hand. Could he ever make her understand?

Riley raised his index finger. "You left." Raised the next finger. "You didn't call." Raised the next finger. "You didn't write." Raised a fourth finger. "You never came back, not even for Christmas." Putting his hand down, he asked. "Is there another name for that I haven't heard?"

Acen frowned. Riley was holding no punches on this conversation. "Okay. You're right. You think I don't know that?"

Riley shrugged, taking a swig of tea, ice rattling

against the glass jar. "How would I know what you know?" He shook his head. "Like I said, I've always tried not to take sides. But she is my sister. My twin sister. You're my best friend. I've been in a tough spot all these years not talking to either of you about the other one. Just trying to keep everything on the back burner. And here you come, riding back into town to stir up all those old memories." He pushed a hand through his hair. "She's not the same girl you left. She stayed. She built a life here. Doesn't mean she's not still hurt."

Acen leaned back, the porch railing creaking beneath him. Being hit with the truth was a bitch. "Point taken. I came back for a lot of reasons. Mostly for my dad. But let's be real. With my knee blown out, I can't play pro ball anymore and I'm not sure what I'm going to do going forward. Who wouldn't come home under those circumstances? And honestly? What do I have to offer any woman at this point? I've got a lot to figure out."

He sighed in frustration at the cards fate had dealt him, then cast a look at his friend. Hating that Rose was so much on his mind when other things needed to be on the front burner at this point. Giving in to his feelings, he asked, "How is she really? No b.s."

Riley tilted his head, sizing up his friend and the information, then relented. "Tougher. Stubborn. Quieter than she used to be. I think she buried a lot more than people realize."

"She looked good," Acen said before he could stop himself. Remembering the long auburn ponytail swirling over her shoulders at practice earlier made his gut cramp with memories. Too bad she'd been wearing sunglasses. But memory supplied the deep blue shade for him.

"Yep. And she knows it," Riley said with a grin. "She runs the women's softball team now. Got the best rec-league record in the region."

"Yeah," Acen said quietly. "I saw that today. She always did have a good arm," Acen said, a soft smile tugging at his mouth.

"Better now. You should see her pitch. Like watching a storm gather." He gave his friend a hard look. "Keep that in mind if you piss her off. She can throw a mean punch as well."

Acen was quiet for a beat. "I didn't expect her to still… get to me like that."

"Yeah," Riley said, his voice going softer. "She does that."

The porch creaked again, and Acen looked out over the yard, where a line of fireflies had started blinking between the hedges. The air was heavy with particular June stillness, the kind that felt like it was holding its breath. Somewhere, a train horn carried faintly over the hills.

"Briana's back too," Riley said, almost as an afterthought.

Acen stiffened. "What?"

"She got in two weeks ago. Been staying at her sister's place off County Road 6. Didn't think it was my news to tell. I haven't told Rose either."

He sighed. "And there will be hell to pay when she finds out I knew and kept it to myself. And I thought she has enough to juggle with you being here. Briana said she wouldn't be coming into town. She's been going to Corinth when she needs to shop. But I know eventually she and Rose will come face-to-face. I most likely should tell Rose tonight. But the timing really sucks on all of this."

Acen muttered something under his breath that wasn't fit for polite company. "But you're telling me." He took a big drink of tea, giving himself a minute to process the news. "What's she doing back?"

Riley shrugged. "Something about a remote job and needing a reset. But don't worry. She hasn't come around looking for you."

Yet. The word didn't need to be said.

Acen set his tea down and rubbed the back of his neck. "What a welcome home."

Riley leaned forward, placing his jar of sweet tea on the floor. "What happened graduation night? Were you sneaking around with Briana for a while?"

Acen shook his head, pushed up off the railing and paced the length of the porch. "It was all so long ago. And so stupid. I didn't have a thing for Briana. I didn't even know the kiss was going to happen. She followed me outside and the next thing I knew she had a lip lock on me. And, hey, I was an eighteen-year-old guy. When a woman throws herself at you like that you go with the flow, right?"

"Seems to me that you could have exercised a little restraint, my friend." Riley leaned forward, elbows on his knees. "I thought you and Rose had an understanding back then."

Acen sighed. "Yea. We did. Sort of. But, I was scared. Heading off to college, big scholarship in the works, lots of pressure. So, I guess I messed up in a moment of weakness."

Riley gave Acen a hard look. "Why didn't you explain to Rose? Make it right before you left?"

Acen winced. "Like I said. I was scared. And, maybe, I wanted to be free on some level. You know, sow some wild oats before making a lifetime commitment."

"I think you were just being selfish." He held up a hand to stop the words he could see waiting to spill from Acen's lips. "I'm not saying you were wrong or right. Just, maybe you should be clear in your own mind why you did what you did before you go trying to get back into Rose's life."

"I'm going to offer to help her coach her team to the state finals."

Tea spewed from Riley's lip as he coughed up the liquid he'd just sipped. "You're *what*?"

Acen crossed his arms over his chest. "You heard me. I'm going to offer to help her with the team."

Riley stopped coughing. Red faced from the exertion, he said, "Have you lost your mind? Did you not hear a word I've said about her? She built that team from nothing. She's a great coach. You don't need to get up in the middle of that and throw her off her coaching game."

"Christ. What a mess." Acen muttered.

"You wanted to come back," Riley said, not unkindly. "Just remember what you're walking into."

"I came back for my dad. That hasn't changed."

Riley gave him a long look. "You came back for more than that. Whether you admit it or not. Just make sure you don't hurt her again."

Acen didn't answer. He didn't need to.

CHAPTER THREE

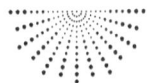

"Let's run it again, ladies!"

Rose blew her whistle and clapped her hands, her voice sharp and sure despite the heat bearing down on the field. Groans rose from the ladies facing her. She couldn't blame them. Sweat clung to her neck under her messy ponytail, and the late-afternoon sun glared off the metal bleachers, but the team was humming with energy despite the groans. Practices always got more intense in the weeks leading up to the regional invitational, and this year's squad had a real shot at taking the title.

"Ginny! Glove up on the hop this time. Maggie, if you're gonna call it, you *have* to catch it"

"Yes, Coach," came the familiar chorus from the group gathered around her in the dugout.

Rose smirked. "Let's not make me get mean."

"Too late," Tasha muttered, loud enough for a ripple of laughter to follow.

Rose was still grinning when a familiar voice—low and irritatingly warm—floated from behind her.

"You always this tough on your team?"

She froze. Took a breath. Turned around.

Acen Wheeler stood behind the dugout fence, arms slung casually over the rail like he had every right to be there. Like a bad dream that just kept coming back. Dreams made her think about bed, which led to thought of Acen there, which made her temper flare.

"Don't you have a porch to haunt somewhere?" she said in a low voice, ignoring the delighted glances being cast at Acen. Like moths to a candle flame. If only they knew what he was capable of, then they'd think twice about those lecherous looks.

"Okay, ladies. Y'all know the drill. Get on out in the field and put it into practice."

She and Acen watched in silence as the team headed out and took up their positions. Which still left the batter and catcher too close for comfort. Rose edged them over to the bleachers. No point in the whole team knowing her personal business.

"Riley invited me." Acen said as they stopped by the hot metal seats, not daring to sit in the heat and risk burned backsides. He hoped lightning didn't strike him from the clear blue sky for the lie. But maybe Rose would take his proposal better if she thought Riley was on his side.

That made her pause. Surely he hadn't said what she thought he'd said. "He did what?"

"Figured I might help with drills," Acen said, stepping to the side of the dugout out of the direct glare of the sun. "You've got a good lineup, but they're tight on fielding. Thought I'd lend a hand."

Rose narrowed her eyes and kept her distance. "Are you sure he didn't mean you can help with *his* team? I don't recall mentioning I need help with mine." She cast an eye over the girls who were hitting and fielding balls like she'd asked. "*We're* about to compete in the regional invitational, in case you haven't heard. His team is not, so that's the one that needs help."

"I'm sure," Acen said with that infuriating half-smile. "He thinks you're too stubborn to ask for help and the regionals will be tough. At least according to him."

Could her brother have actually set her up like this knowing how she felt about what Acen had done all those years ago? He must have lost his mind if that was the case. She'd never let anyone assistant coach for her before. And if she decided to go that route, Acen Wheeler would be the last person she'd trust to be that for her.

His piercing blue eyes sent a secret shiver down her spine as he gazed at her. She wished she had her sunglasses on and was too proud to put them on now and give him a hint of the turmoil he was creating.

"As you said. Riley's team didn't make regionals, so I

know he meant your team. Look" he pushed a hand through his hair, cut his eyes to the cluster of interested women out on the ball field, and said, "I know this might be a bit awkward, but Riley said you really want to pull off the state championship this year."

And just like that the stench of graduation night rose around them like a dark cloud. Her questions, his lack of answers or any acknowledgment that anything had happened at all for that matter. Did he really think he could just show up back here all these years later and all was forgiven without any words being spoken.

From the pitcher's mound, Ginny called out, "Who's the snack?"

Rose spun on her heel, angry energy coursing through her veins. Lord save her from young, nosy women.

"Focus, Ginny!"

And then felt bad about taking her own emotions out on her pitcher. Ginny looked surprised by the vehement reply to her teasing question and quickly got busy studying her gloved hand. Dammit. She didn't need this emotional trauma floating around in her head.

Acen chuckled, bringing her attention back to him. "Glad to know I haven't lost *all* my charm."

"Keep talking and you might." She snapped.

But she was already calculating. The girls *did* need help if they were going to make it to state champions.

And Acen *was* a professional player. That didn't mean she wanted him here. It just meant she had to decide which mattered more: her pride or her team.

After a beat her team won out and she tossed him a glove from the equipment bag at her feet. "You drop *one* ball, and I'm kicking you off this field."

He caught it one-handed, grinning. "Deal."

The next hour passed in a blur of drills, fly balls, and shouted instructions. Rose hated to admit it, but Acen still had it—fluid, confident, encouraging without coddling. The girls responded to him like he was a magic charm, and by the time practice wrapped, they were laughing and high-fiving like they'd won something already.

Rose leaned on the dugout bench, arms crossed, watching him joke with Maggie and Tasha like he'd never left. She ignored the twist in her gut. Nothing good for her heart was going to come from this deal with the devil.

Acen high-fived all around once more and loped to his truck parked in the adjacent lot. Tasha came to the dugout and sat down, nudging her elbow. "So... you gonna keep pretending he's not fine as hell?"

"I can acknowledge a man's face and still want to throw a bucket of Gatorade at it."

"Sure," Tasha said, smirking. "That's healthy."

. . .

WHEN THE PLAYERS HAD CLEARED OUT, ROSE TURNED TO find Acen watching her, glove in hand.

Startled, she glanced around but everyone else was gone. "I thought you left."

"I forgot to ask you about practice scheduling."

"You've still got that arm," she said, nodding toward the diamond.

He shrugged. "Muscle memory."

"Not all muscles forget," she said without thinking.

Silence stretched between them. Not tense exactly —but heavy. Loaded.

"You were good with them," she said finally, brushing a hand over her arm like it could wipe the past off her skin.

"I missed this," he said softly. "Not just the game. The people. You."

Rose looked away. "You don't get to say that like nothing happened."

"I know."

"You left, Acen. You didn't just choose Briana. You *left*. And I had to stay here and—"

"I know."

His voice was quiet. Steady. And it hurt worse because he didn't argue.

"I thought about you every day," he added. "Still do."

Rose's breath caught.

But before she could answer, Riley's voice rang out from behind the bleachers.

"Hey! You two gonna make out or kill each other? I'm taking bets."

Rose rolled her eyes. "Neither. Practice is over."

She turned her back to Acen and headed toward her truck, heart thudding against her ribs like it had twenty years ago—only louder.

CHAPTER FOUR

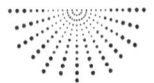

Thursday at five, Rose locked the door to the Southern Sips coffee shop and headed out to meet some of the team for supper. Sleep had been elusive last night after the prolonged practice session with Acen pushing the girls to their limits. And pushing her emotions to the limit as well. She *had* to get a grip on herself if she was going to survive until the playoffs were over. Hopefully with a big regional trophy as her reward for doing the right thing for the team.

The dining room at Fin to Fork smelled like fried catfish, fresh cornbread, and a week's worth of gossip. Spotting her friends already seated, Rose slid into the booth next to Tasha, while Maggie, Ginny, and Dani crowded the opposite bench, looking over the menu even though they always had the catfish special.

"Y'all, I swear," Ginny said, fanning herself with a

laminated menu, "Coach Rose has got us out there training like we're headed to the Olympics."

"That's because you keep ducking fly balls like they're angry bees," Rose said, arching a brow.

"She's not wrong," Maggie muttered.

"Anyway," Tasha said with a grin, "let's get to the real topic. Namely, Acen Wheeler's biceps."

Dani groaned. "Here we go."

Rose raised a hand. "No. Absolutely not. We're not turning supper into a slow descent into thirst."

Tasha leaned in, eyes sparkling. "Just saying. For a man his age—"

"We're all his age!" Rose snapped, cheeks heating.

"Not me," Ginny chimed in. "Which means there's still hope for me if I get dumped by my current honey."

Rose shook her head. At twenty-five Ginny sometimes made her feel ancient. She reached for her sweet tea, took a sip to give everyone a beat to realize she meant business. "We're here to talk strategy, remember? The invitational bracket came out this morning. And we need to get serious."

"It feels like we've been pretty serious already. I know I've got sore muscles to prove it." Tasha said but added a smile and a wink to show she wasn't being snarky.

They'd been friends for so long Rose knew Tasha was sending her a chill vibe. And maybe she deserved it. She'd been pushing everyone hard. And with the addition of Acen, they'd pushed harder. The team would give their all and she knew that. It was good to have a friend who could subtly call you out when needed.

"Strategize all you want," Maggie said, opening her phone. "I already saw we're playing Madison County's team first. And that's one tough team."

The Madison Marauders were certainly a good team, but Rose believed the Pirate Queens could beat them.

She was about to say so when the door opened and the whole energy of the room shifted. Conversations stopped, forks stopped clattering on plates.

Into the silence stepped a tall man in a navy polo and dark jeans, his sun-kissed blond hair tousled just enough to look accidental. He had that clean, out-of-town look—like he hadn't grown up enduring high humidity that left you feeling like you were breathing through a wet rag or learning to say *sir* and *ma'am* by the age of five. His eyes were green and curious, and when he glanced around the restaurant, he smiled like the whole place was a warm joke he was glad to be in on. He stopped at the checkout counter and spoke to Diane.

Rose saw Diane nod in their direction. What could be going on?

She glanced around taking in the stranger's effect on the diners. Old Amos and Sarah Donovan had a reserved look on their faces. Not surprising considering that in a town this small if you couldn't claim kin at *least* three generations back you were considered an outsider. Amos and Sarah both could claim kin back to the eighteen hundreds on all side and considered themselves to be the authorities on who belonged - and who didn't. It could really get on a person's nerves after a while. All that judginess.

A table of weekenders who must have arrived a day early looked curious. Like they were wondering how this hot guy had stumbled into this little establishment. Rose knew them from her coffee shop. Cindy and James were friendly. Valerie and Sam not so much. The females looked interest. And who could blame them?

"Who's *that*?" Ginny whispered.

Rose found herself staring at the stranger for a second too long.

"*That*," Dani said, leaning across the table, "is Declan Rowe. He moved into the old Langley place last week. Came in for a tire rotation and ended up talking my Uncle Joe's ear off about vet care and boarding."

"Hot *and* an animal lover," Tasha murmured. "The Lord is testing me."

"Tasha! Seriously?" Rose asked, arching an eyebrow.

"Definitely serious." Tasha responded, licking her lips.

Rose glanced over to see if the man in question was watching the interplay at their table and seen Tasha's move. Luckily, she got only a view of his broad shoulders tapering to a narrow waist and a very nice backside.

As if on cue, Declan turned and caught sight of their table. His eyes landed on Rose. His smile widened.

Rose felt her cheeks heat and cursed her fair complexion that made blushes stand out all the more. Maybe she could blame it on the heat.

"Uh-oh," Maggie muttered. "He's coming over."

Rose barely had time to stop berating herself for the blush before Declan approached. Every eye in the place tracked his movements and Rose knew they'd be a hot topic of conversation later. But Declan acted like he didn't notice.

"Excuse me," he said, voice smooth and Southern with a lilt that hinted he wasn't from *this* part of the South. "Mind if I interrupt?"

Tasha smiled. "Interrupt away."

Declan turned to the table a few feet away with an unoccupied chair. "May I borrow this chair?"

Of course, it was the table where Amos and Sarah were sitting, eyes still glued to the stranger in their midst. Rose held her breath. Amos nodded to Roses's relief. And surprise.

Declan smiled, placing the chair at the end of the booth table. "I'm still learning the lay of the land. Diane at the counter mentioned this was the famous Pickwick Pirate Queens. Women's league champs?"

"That's us," Maggie said proudly.

Rose raised a brow. "You a fan of slow-pitch softball?"

"I'm a fan of team sports, community engagement… and charming company."

He looked at her when he said it. Rose felt the warmth bloom up her neck again and immediately hated how her heart skipped a beat.

"Well," Rose said slowly, "we're just grabbing supper, but you're welcome to join us. If you don't mind sitting next to the loud one."

"I'm not *that* loud," Tasha said.

"You are," said the entire table.

Declan laughed and scooted his chair closer to the table, his cologne faint and woodsy, like cedar and something wild.

So much for discussing game strategy. A stranger at the table might mean a spy. She laughed silently at herself. *Get a grip McAlister. This isn't a world series level game. No one is here to steal your playbook.* But still maybe she needed a distraction. The girls obviously thought she was way too tense about the upcoming games.

"I'm Declan Rowe," he said, holding out a hand. "New guy in town."

"Rose McAllister," she said, shaking it. "Coach. Local."

"I gathered." His eyes held hers for a second too long. "You look familiar for some reason." Then he laughed. "Wow. That sounded like the worst pick up line in history. But you do look familiar."

"Was Riley McAlister your real estate agent?" Tasha asked.

Declan moved his gaze from Rose to Tasha. "Yes."

"That explains it then. Rose and Riley are twins."

Declan returned his gaze to Rose. "Is that right? Coach. Twin. What other interesting things should I know about you? For example, do you need a sponsor for your team?"

And just like that, for the first time in a very long time, Acen Wheeler wasn't the only man in town who made her feel like something was about to happen.

An hour later the group stood in the hot parking lot where heat waves shimmied off the asphalt like wavy ghosts.

"I'll be in touch about that sponsorship." Declan said to Rose, taking her hand.

"I appreciate it." Rose said, letting her hand linger in his grip. "We're always in need of funds to keep us going. The Southern Sips Coffee Shop is mine and I'm there six days a week till five. Stop by any time."

Declan said his goodbyes to the others and sauntered to his car. Five pairs of eyes glued to the ass of his nicely fitting jeans.

"Whoo-ee!" Tasha said, expressing everyone's thoughts. "That is one fine piece of maleness. Smooth moves. And he has an eye for you Rose. Unfortunately for me."

CHAPTER FIVE

The afternoon heat had started to burn off, but the air at the Wheeler garage was thick enough to cut with a socket wrench. The smell of grease and oil mingled with other less identifiable smells. All of them woven throughout his growing up so that anytime, anywhere he smelled them he was transported instantly back here to his dad's garage no matter his physical location at the time.

Joe Wheeler had made a life and a living fixing friends, and strangers, cars for fifty years. Acen had been his father's right-hand man during his teen years. Before the big baseball scholarship that had changed his life. He held back a bitter laugh about that. One wrong move. One moment in time. That's all it took for his career to go down the drain in a heartbeat.

Wiping the sweat from his brow, he ducked out from under the lifted hood of a dusty Silverado. He could feel someone staring. Sure enough, Riley leaned against the workbench, arms crossed, grinning like a man who'd just caught his brother in a lie.

"So," Riley said, cracking open a soda he held. "You hear about Declan Rowe yet?"

Acen gave him a flat look. "What about him?"

"New guy in town. Handsome. Polite. *Real* friendly. Had supper with Rose and some of the girls at Fin to Fork yesterday. The catfish special. Or so I heard. You know how that goes around here. Might be one hundred percent true. Might be less than one hundred percent. I just thought you should know. In case you aren't tuned back into the local grapevine yet."

Acen's jaw clenched. "That so?"

"Sat next to her, too," Riley added, clearly enjoying himself. "Word is he asked Diane for her name specifically. Told her he liked team sports and charming company."

Acen grunted, reaching for a wrench. "Sounds like a line."

"Maybe. But Rose smiled."

He didn't mean for it to get under his skin. Really, he didn't.

It wasn't like he had any claim to her. Not anymore.

Still, the thought of some shiny stranger sliding into her life, making her laugh the way he used to—it made something low in his chest twist like a pulled muscle.

Riley smirked. "You jealous?"

He hid his face from his friend by applying the

wrench to a trouble spot under the hood. It gave unexpectedly and he grunted a bit, then answered. "Not my business who she eats supper with."

"That's not a no."

Acen didn't answer. He slammed the hood shut harder than necessary.

Riley let him stew for a second before adding, "He's bought the Langley house."

"So you are the realtor for Mr. Handsome and didn't see fit to tell me this information before now?"

Riley squinted. "I sell real estate to handsome men all the time. Beautiful women too. But none of them have made a play for my sister. I'm just keeping you in the loop, so to speak. He's a veterinarian. Most likely planning to stay around full time for a long time."

"A vet?" Acen snorted. "Must be some kind of specialty vet that doesn't get dirty."

"What's that supposed to mean?"

"Nothing. Just... he's probably one of those guys who wears scarves when it's eighty degrees and drinks herbal tea in mason jars."

"Sounds like you're making up stories 'cause he's prettier than you."

Acen shot him a glare. "He's not prettier than me."

"You keep telling yourself that," Riley said, laughing as he walked away.

. . .

THAT EVENING, ACEN FOUND HIMSELF BACK AT THE BALL field in an attempt to shake unwanted images from his head. The light was fading, the sky soaked in oranges and pinks. He stopped in his tracks, gaze drawn to a lone figure on the field.

Realizing who it was, he gave a low curse.

Rose stood on the pitcher's mound with a bucket of balls at her feet making underhanded tosses into the net set up a few feet away. One. Two. Three. Steady as a metronome the balls went into the net

He should just walk away. But when had he ever done the should haves? His feet carried him quietly across the distance separating them.

"Didn't know you took batting practice alone." He said in a quiet voice.

She didn't flinch in surprise or even look up. "Didn't know you started stalking people."

Acen chuckled. "Call it… monitoring."

"You get lost on the way to minding your own business?"

He stepped into her peripheral vision, hands in his pockets. "Look, I didn't come here to fight."

"Then you've got terrible timing."

He paused, toeing the edge of the mound. "I heard about your supper with the new guy."

She stopped tossing. "Declan?"

"That his name?"

She looked at him, brows lifted. "You jealous?"

"Nope," he said, way too fast.

She smirked. "He's nice. Smart. Funny. Handsome."

Acen's jaw tightened. "You forgot charming."

"Oh, he's that too," she said lightly. "I guess Riley has been filling your ears with tales if you know that much. Or, if not Riley specifically, then the town grapevine. Assuming you're tuned back into it that is."

Silence stretched between them. The sun slipped lower.

Tension flowed across the space like a living cord.

"I'm not here to play games, Rose," Acen said finally. "You want me gone, I'll stay out of your way. But if you don't…"

"If I don't?" she echoed, her voice quieter now.

"Then maybe we stop pretending twenty years changed everything when it really didn't."

Her breath caught.

She looked at him—really looked. The same stubborn set of his shoulders. The faint scar on his chin from that summer they fell off Riley's four-wheeler. The eyes she used to dream about and now hated dreaming of.

"I don't know what I want, Acen," she said honestly. "I'm still trying to figure that out."

He nodded once. "Fair enough."

She picked up another softball and turned back to the net. "You know how to hit, don't you?"

He grinned. "Still do."

"Then get in the cage."

He picked up a bat from the bag lying next to the

dugout and took his position just as the automatic field lights clicked on bathing them both in a spotlight.

And just like that, they were back on familiar ground—two kids who knew how to throw heat and take it, even if the game had changed.

CHAPTER SIX

Rose was still angry at herself for how easily Declan had charmed her Thursday evening.

And worse—for how much she'd *liked* it.

She wasn't a woman who needed flirting. She had responsibilities, a team, a house to maintain, a twin brother who still treated her like his little sister even if they were born four minutes apart.

She didn't have time for two men circling like bees around honeysuckle.

She pushed open the door to the feed store too hard and made the bell jangle like a fire alarm. The Saturday shoppers stopped and looked at her.

Blushing, she held up a hand and laughed. "Sorry! No need for alarm. Just me barging in out of nowhere."

Charlie Martin chucked. "The way that bell went off I thought for sure there was a town emergency."

"Nope. Just me coming in to ask for sponsorship

money for the team." She winked at him. "You wouldn't want to contribute, would you?"

Charlie smiled. "Why, Rose. Are you soliciting me? And me a county deputy. And a married man, too."

Everyone nearby laughed out loud, and Rose's blush deepened. Her cheeks might just set off the smoke alarm after all.

"Well, are you open to that?" She teased, playing along despite the blush. "Championships don't come cheap, you know."

Charlie reached for his wallet. "Just teasin' you, Rose. I'm happy to contribute to the Pickwick Pirate Queens taking the championship trophy." He handed her a twenty. "Sorry it's not more."

"Charlie, we're grateful for help from anyone regardless of the amount." She tucked the bill into her pocket.

From her position behind the cash register, Shelly Burke said, "Rose, Mr. Campbell was expecting you to come in. He's going to sponsor new shirts for the team for the playoffs. He's back in his office."

As Rose made her way through the store, friends and neighbors pressed bills into her hands as they passed her in the big aisle leading to the back. "Stop, y'all. I need to write all this down so I can thank everyone properly for the donations."

"Just win that championship for us. That'll be thanks enough." Said Amos Sanders as he pressed yet another bill into her hand. She gave him a hug.

"Thank you so much, Mr. Sanders! And no pressure, right?" She laughed. So did the others but it was good-natured teasing. "I'll do the best I can and so will the team."

"Of course there's pressure. That's part of my hard-earned social security in your hand." He put a gnarled hand on her shoulder and smiled to show he didn't mean it. "I don't doubt you, Rose. You always do what you say you will and if there's a way you can make it happen, I'm sure it will. You ladies enjoy yourselves. Winning the championship is a wonderful thing, but there will be other years if you don't. Trust me. I've seen a lot of em,"

"Hey, Josh." Rose said as she finally stood in the doorway to the office. "Shelly said you were lookin' for me to come in today."

Josh looked up, his hair in disarray and eyes slightly unfocused. He shook his head, and his eyes came in focus, but the hair remained in disarray. Rose smiled to herself.

Typical for Josh who had no time for fooling with things like how his hair looked. He was the bane of his wife Carol's existence. She was forever trying to get him to at least run a comb through the mess. And took him regularly to the Cut and Run to get a trim. But Josh looked good with his messy hair and thick glasses. Just like the nerdy nice guy he'd always been.

He pushed his glasses up and smiled. "Rose. Glad

you came in. I wanted to talk to you about new team shirts for the championship tournament."

"Now, Josh. You already paid for the shirts we're wearing, and they got us to the playoffs. Don't you think we might lose our mojo if we changed to new shirts at this point?"

Josh frowned. "I hadn't thought about it from that angle to tell you the truth. I'm just so proud of y'all for making it to the playoffs I wanted you to have some really nice new shirts to whoop some ass in during the tournament."

"I really appreciate that, Josh. But I think we'll stick with the shirts we've worn all season." She laughed. "I guess I'm more superstitious than I thought. And maybe some of the girls are as well now that I think about it. Ginny's socks have been pretty funky smelling lately."

Josh laughed with her. "Okay. But the offer is on the table any time you want to circle back to me on it."

Rose made her way back to the front of the store and stopped to talk to Shelly.

"So, are you getting new shirts for the playoffs? Y'all have had that same design for years. Don't you think you should do a special one just for these games? You know, so everyone will know you're in the playoffs when you wear them around town. Something current and jazzy." Shelly was all about new designs and current trends.

"Nope. We're keeping the same shirts we've played

in all season. I wouldn't want to mess up our luck by changing them at this point."

Shelly's eye got round. "Oh wow! I didn't think about that. You surely don't want to mess up your luck at this point." She reached into her pocket and brought out a round silver metal piece. "This is my lucky quarter. I have it with me all the time I know it doesn't look like a quarter anymore." She rubbed it between her index finger and thumb. "I've worn all the markings off over the years. It's from the year I was born. My mama gave it to me when I was sixteen. She said I needed all the luck I could get with my attitude and wayward ways."

They laughed together.

"Well, it seems to have worked pretty well for you. A husband that adores you and two beautiful kids."

Shelly smiled and put the much-worn quarter back in her pocket.

"You're right about that. I'm truly blessed"

The heat outside had her hurrying to her truck where she found a note tucked under her windshield wiper when she came out of the feed store. It was written in sharp, clean handwriting on thick, cream-colored stationery—because of course Declan Rowe used *stationery*.

Rose—

Supper with the girls was fun. I'd love to take you out sometime—just the two of us. I hear the food at The Silver Catfish is legendary. Say yes.

—Declan

She stared at the note for a full thirty seconds, then turned it over, half expecting there to be a pressed flower or a wax seal on the back. It seemed like his style. Cosmopolitan. Not like the local guys she'd known all her life. Honest, hardworking. Not fancy. But full of heart and good guys all he same. There wasn't a pressed flower or a wax seal. And somehow it felt a little disappointing.

She glanced around the parking lot. No one was looking in her direction. And why would they be? It was a normal day for everyone. Including her. No need to read anything earth shattering into this.

She needed time to think over her response. Hadn't she just been thinking earlier that she didn't need guys in her life right now? Still, she'd make sure she was in a quiet place with plenty of time to think before answering. Maybe the Universe was sending her a message. Maybe it was time to be interested in someone. Someone cosmopolitan. Someone so outside her usual life that no echoes of the past would intrude.

She slid the note into her bag and climbed into the truck, heart beating a little faster than she cared to admit. Declan was thoughtful, and steady, and—so far —uncomplicated.

But her stomach twisted as she pulled out of the parking lot, because nothing in Pickwick Bend ever stayed uncomplicated for long.

CHAPTER SEVEN

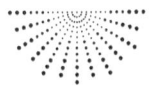

Across town, Acen was elbow-deep in grease and regret when the past walked right through the open garage bay door in three-inch heels and a designer blouse that had no business being this close to a carburetor. Or in this town for that matter. Not on a bright Saturday afternoon.

Cursing silently, he stepped back from the car. At least Riley had given him a heads-up so that he wasn't totally taken by surprise. He'd have preferred to run into her at the local Piggly Wiggly in front of half the town to this though. This felt calculated on her part. And he didn't have time for her calculation in his life these days. He'd let her screw up his future once because he'd been young and dumb. Older and wiser – and lesson learned – was the order of the day now.

"Briana," he said flatly, yanking off his gloves and keeping his distance. "Can I help you?"

"I hope so." She flashed a smile that didn't reach her eyes. "My check engine light came on. Thought I'd bring it to someone who actually knows how to fix things."

He crossed his arms. Apparently, the lack of enthusiasm in his voice hadn't clicked with her.. "You passed three shops on the way here."

"I wanted to see how you're settling back in." She tossed her head in a well-remembered move. It made her smooth blonde hair shimmer just below her chin drawing attention to her long slim neck.

Too bad for her that it didn't work on him anymore. "You don't care how I'm settling in."

Briana's smile faded. "That's not fair."

"What's not fair is you showing up after twenty years like you left on a lunch break."

Her expression flickered - guilt, maybe. Or annoyance at being read so easily. "Look, I didn't come here to fight."

"Then say what you need to say."

She stepped closer, voice softer, put her hand on his arm. "You and I... we had history, Acen. I just thought maybe, now that we're both back, we could talk. See where things stand."

Acen stepped back, letting her hand fall away. "Nothing stands, Briana. Whatever we had ended a long time ago. You and I... we were a mistake."

She flinched. "That's harsh."

"It's true."

She looked away, then back again, eyes sharper now. "So this is about *her*, isn't it?"

"You know damn well it's always been about her."

Briana's jaw tightened, but she nodded like she'd been expecting it. "You're still chasing Rose McAllister after all these years? You really think she'll ever forgive you?"

He didn't answer. He didn't need to.

Briana laughed - quiet, bitter. "Good luck with that. Small towns don't forget. And neither does she."

Then she turned and stepped away, heels clicking across the concrete like punctuation marks on a sentence she'd written years ago.

She turned at the door. "She'll never take you back. And we had a good thing once upon a time. This isn't over, Acen."

THAT NIGHT, ROSE SAT ON HER PORCH SWING, THE moonlight silvering the edges of her thoughts.

She still hadn't responded to Declan's note. The food at The Silver Catfish *was* legendary, and part of her wanted to go. To try. To let someone new in.

But every time she thought about it, she saw Acen's face. Not just how he looked now—but how he'd looked back then. At eighteen, leaning against the hood of Riley's car, telling her he was leaving. Telling her he loved *her*, even though he had kissed Briana, but he was going anyway.

And then the weeks. The silence. The long, hollow years.

She closed her eyes, gripping the swings' chain until her fingers ached.

Her phone buzzed. A message from Declan:

Still hoping for a yes.

She stared at it for a long time.

Then typed: *Dinner sounds nice. Tomorrow?*

She hit send before she could change her mind.

Let the past stay where it belonged.

CHAPTER EIGHT

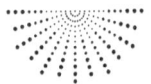

The Silver Catfish wasn't fancy by city standards, but for Pickwick Bend, it was as close to date-night elegant as it got. Tucked against the curve of the river, the restaurant boasted an old-fashioned porch, stone fireplace, checkered table-cloths, and the best house made slaw this side of the Mississippi.

She'd texted Declan earlier in the day asking to meet him at the restaurant. Team practice had run late. And she'd still had the smell of Acen in her mind when she went home. So, she'd made the request, Delcan had replied yes but with concern about why, and she'd showered Acen right out of her mind. She hoped.

Declan stood when stood when she walked in.

She hadn't worn anything fancy—just jeans and a fitted navy blouse—but the way his eyes lingered made her feel like she'd stepped off a movie screen.

"You look..." He hesitated, then smiled. "Exactly how I hoped."

Rose arched an eyebrow. "So—tired from work and practice and mildly skeptical about the playoffs?"

Declan laughed, offering his arm. "Come on, Coach. Let me feed you something fried and delicious."

She let him lead her to a table by the window, where the light glinted off the water and the cicadas outside hummed their steady Southern chorus.

"I wish I could have come and watched y'all practice today, but the animals were booked solid at my office, and I barely got out in time to clean up myself." His eyes smiled into hers.

"No worries." She answered. 'You'd most likely be a bit bored watching practice. Lot's of yelling and do-overs on plays. Nothing like a real game."

He chucked, and she felt herself relaxing.

"So, you really grew up in Charleston?" she asked, her voice curious but easy.

He nodded, lips quirking up in a half-smile. "Sure did. Big ol' porch, live oaks with moss hanging like laundry lines, humidity so thick you could slice it with a butter knife. Of course, that part isn't much different here. Mama always had sweet tea in the fridge and Motown playing on the radio. That was her favorite. Ask me to sing the words to any of those songs. I can do without even thinking about it."

She laughed. "That sounds nice. We didn't have all that here, but Pickwick Bend's always had its own rhythm. Slower maybe. But sure, and steady. Daddy said it was the kind of town where everybody knew your name and all your business. Like all the other small towns."

He chuckled. "Sounds like home to me."

She smiled. "You chose to come here, remember? Nobody made you."

He looked out over the river a moment before answering. "Yeah, I did. After vet school, I had offers in bigger places—Nashville, Birmingham... even somewhere out in Texas. But none of them felt right. I guess I wanted roots. Not to say there aren't roots in Charleston. Those are some *very* deep roots there. But it's more formal. You know? I wanted a place where folks still wave when they pass you on the road and care if your dog goes missing. Pickwick Bend had that."

"You really came here for the dogs and the wave-smilin'?"

"Not just that," he said with a grin. "There's something about small towns. The way they hold onto their stories. The way people show up for each other. I figured if I was gonna put down stakes, it should be somewhere that still remembers how to sit on a porch and talk. Plus, on the more practical side, there's the lake. And lower taxes and property costs. And I'm the only vet in town here."

She smiled at that. "Well, you picked right."

He tilted his head. "What about you? Ever think about leaving?"

"Lord, no," she said, shaking her head. "I mean, sure, I've wondered what it'd be like to live in a place where you're not always running into your third-grade teacher or the boy who broke your heart in high school at the Piggly Wiggly. But Pickwick Bend's in my bones. I have my own house. And the coffee shop. And my team. Those girls? They drive me half-crazy, forget their gloves, argue over the lineup—but they've got more heart than sense, and I wouldn't trade them for anything. And friends I've known since birth...or at least school. And as much as I complain about everybody knowing everybody's business, there's comfort in that. In knowing there are multiple people who will go out of their way to help me if I need it. Just because we're an extended family. You can't get that in the city."

She paused for breath. "Good grief. Listen to me going on and on about all this. You must be regretting asking me to dinner about now."

He leaned in, eyes intent on her face, listening.

Not nodding politely or glancing at his phone like most folks did these days—but really listening. Like her words mattered. Like he was collecting each one and tucking it away somewhere safe.

It made her pause. Made her feel seen.

"You're not just waiting for your turn to talk, are you?" she asked, almost teasing, almost amazed.

"No, ma'am," he said. "I'm hearing you."

And Lord help her, that might've been the rarest thing of all.

Then their catfish arrived, golden and steaming, and giving her the excuse to break eye contact with him. This was getting a little more intense than she'd expected. She forked up a mouthful of succulent, tender catfish and almost moaned. It was that good.

Declan leaned in and asked, "What made you say yes?"

Rose blinked, coming back to reality at the table. "To dinner?"

He nodded.

She thought about it, and decided honesty was the best policy. "You asked nicely. And I figured I could use a distraction."

He didn't press. Just smiled. "Well, I hope I'm a good one."

And for the most part—he was.

But as she sipped sweet tea, she tried to ignore the ache creeping in behind her ribs.

Declan was good company. Thoughtful. Attractive. Present.

He made her laugh. Made her think.

But as the check arrived and he reached for his wallet, she found herself wondering—*is this what peace feels like, or just the absence of pain?*

He walked her to her truck, his hand brushing hers. He paused beside the driver's side door, eyes searching hers.

"Can I see you again?" he asked.

Rose hesitated. Then nodded. "Yeah. I think I'd like that."

He leaned in - not quite a kiss. Just close enough to feel his breath, smell the faint pine of his cologne. Then he pulled back and smiled.

"Goodnight, Rose."

"Night, Declan."

She climbed into her truck, heart thudding - not from what had happened, but from everything that hadn't.

She drove home slowly, the stars scattered above her like questions with no easy answers.

But out in the parking lot, leaning against a truck that didn't belong to him, Acen Wheeler watched through the shadows.

He hadn't meant to drive by.

Honestly. And he blamed Riley for mentioning that Rose had a date tonight and where she would be.

He'd told himself he was just taking the truck for a drive to make sure that carburetor repair was working right before handing the truck back to the owner. Told himself that he'd just happened to take the long way – even though The Silver Catfish was at the end of a very long dead-end road he had no business being on tonight. That turning into the lot was about needing to check a slight rattle under the hood.

But when he saw Rose—her head tilted back in

laughter, Declan's hand resting casually on her arm, both of them glowing in the light of the full moon overhead—it was like something inside him cracked wide open.

He'd seen her smile a thousand times.

But not like that.

That smile was soft. Unburdened. Hopeful.

And it wasn't for him.

Acen clenched his jaw, swallowed the bitterness rising in his throat, and turned away.

He wasn't sure which hurt more—the fact that Rose was moving on… or the gut-deep fear that maybe she *should*.

He waited until he was sure her truck had disappeared on the highway home before he cranked up his own and rolled into the night with his own twisted thoughts his only company.

CHAPTER NINE

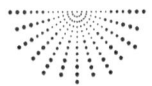

The parking lot of The Mimosa Tree Diner was packed when Rose pulled in and circled for the third time, her old Ford grumbling like it had better places to be. It was eight o'clock on the dot, and every single space looked like it had been claimed since sunrise. She sighed and found a narrow spot between a pickup truck with two muddy fishing poles hanging out the bed and a compact car covered in bumper stickers from Dollywood and SEC football.

"Uh oh," she muttered under her breath. "How heavy has the rumor mill been churning this morning?"

She glanced at her reflection in the rearview mirror —hair frizzing just slightly from the June humidity, eyes a little wary. She didn't *think* she looked like someone who'd caused a town-wide stir, but that was the thing about Pickwick Bend—you never had to actually *do* much to become the center of attention.

Still, The Mimosa Tree was *always* packed at breakfast, even this late in the morning. Maybe this was just the regular morning crowd—retirees holding court by the window booths, moms in yoga pants, and the usual mess of old men in John Deere hats arguing over who had the better tomatoes this year.

Maybe it wasn't about her.

Maybe it was just in her head. Maybe her own mixed-up, tangled-up feelings were making her sensitive.

But the minute she stepped through the door and the bell overhead jingled, a hush fell over the diner like someone had hit the pause button on a jukebox.

Every single eye in the place turned toward her— Miss Myrna with her bright pink lipstick holding a church bulletin she'd been about to pin on the bulletin board, Junior Harlan with his suspenders and his suspicious glare, even little Maylee Parsons, who stopped coloring her placemat and whispered something to her mama.

Okay. *Maybe* it was about her this time.

The girls were already gathered at their usual table in the back corner—heads together like conspirators, mugs full of steaming coffee, and matching smirks that had trouble written all over 'em. It made Rose wish she'd just stayed at her own coffee shop and nursed a mug of drip brew in peace. Maybe she should start offering something more substantial than cookies and muffins over there.

"Well, well, *well*," Maggie drawled, tilting her mug in a mock salute. "If it ain't our very own belle of the ball."

Rose sighed and slid into the empty seat beside Dani, her shoulder brushing against the familiar vinyl booth. "I'm not in the mood."

"Oh, sweetie," Tasha said, eyes twinkling. "You brought this on yourself when you went to The Silver Catfish wearin' your hair-down blouse."

"My *what*?"

"You know the one," Tasha said, gesturing vaguely. "That navy button-up. The one that makes your hair look all glossy and movie-star perfect. That auburn against navy? Mercy, it's downright *criminal*."

Rose blinked. "Y'all are exhausting."

"By six this morning, half of Pickwick Bend had already heard about your little dinner date," Dani added with a giggle. "By seven, the other half had an opinion about it."

Rose gave her a withering look just as Allie came bustling over with a bunch of menus in hand. Her apron was slightly askew, and she had a pencil tucked behind each ear like she meant business.

"Well *good* mornin', Rose," Allie said with a grin. "Tell me about the new man in your life."

That earned a chorus of laughter from the table and more than a few amused glances from neighboring booths. Mrs. Edna Harper in the corner even leaned in, not bothering to hide her interest.

Allie winked. "Guess you're gettin' the third degree this morning, huh?"

Rose took a menu and nodded grimly. "An FBI interrogation would be a step up, honestly."

"Come on now," Tasha said. "You couldn't have *really* thought you'd go on a date in *Pickwick Bend* and nobody'd find out. Especially not at The Silver Catfish. That place has more windows than the Baptist church."

Rose sighed and handed her menu back. "I don't even know why you bring menus to us, Allie. We order the same thing every time."

Allie collected them with a chuckle as everyone else held theirs up like white flags. "Habit, I guess. You never know when somebody might surprise me."

"You're tone's saying you're not talking about breakfast orders," Rose muttered.

"You look happy," Ginny added, her voice softer than the others. "Word is Declan opened the truck door for you."

"That's... not scandalous."

"It is around here," Maggie said with a smirk. "Last man who opened a car door was my cousin's boyfriend —and he was trying to beg forgiveness for being a jerk."

Rose rolled her eyes. "He was just being polite. It was *just* dinner."

"Dinner that included hand brushing, parking lot lingering, and a confirmed second date," Dani said, reading off her phone like it was the morning news.

"Straight from April Sue, who was working the hostess stand."

Rose's mouth dropped. "She *posted* that?"

"Group text," Dani corrected. "But you know how that spreads."

Rose groaned and buried her face in her hands. "Lord, just kill me."

"Too late," Tasha teased, patting her hand. "You're already in love."

"I am *not.*"

"But you like him," Ginny said, eyes searching her face. "Don't you?"

Rose hesitated, fingers still pressed to her cheeks. "I like that he's... easy. No baggage. No ghosts."

But even as she said it, her heart gave a little stutter. One that had nothing to do with coffee.

And everything to do with possibility.

Pushing away the feelings, she swirled her hands in the air. "Enough, y'all. Can we just eat breakfast in peace? And talk about fishing or boating or anything else that someone can think of?"

"You can change the subject all you want," Tasha said. "But it won't change what everyone's thinking about."

Rose sighed because truer words were never spoken.

CHAPTER TEN

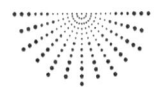

Acen stood behind the garage, pacing a slow trench into the gravel with the heel of his boots. The June sun was already stretching its fingers across the sky, hot and unrelenting even this early in the morning. The air smelled like oil, sun-warmed metal, and the faint sweetness of honeysuckle drifting from the hedges along the edge of the lot. Crickets chirped lazily in the high grass near the fence line, and somewhere down the road, a dog barked at nothing.

He shoved his hands in his pockets, then yanked them back out, frustrated. He couldn't get the image out of his head—Rose, laughing in that way she did when she was truly at ease. Rose, looking at *him*—*that man*, Declan, the way she used to look at *Acen*—like he was the only one in the room. Like she hadn't been burned before.

He swallowed hard and kicked a loose rock, sending it skittering across the gravel. Dust rose in a lazy puff and drifted away. He'd told himself he was done. That he'd said what he needed to say, offered his apology like a grown man should, and left the rest in her hands.

But watching her ease into someone else's orbit like it was the most natural thing in the world? That he couldn't stomach.

He paced back the other way, jaw tight.

Around the corner came Riley, rag slung over one shoulder, grease smudged on the edge of his shirt. His boots crunched in the gravel as he approached, his face unreadable except for the glint in his eyes that said he'd seen more than Acen wanted him to.

"Don't you have some real estate to sell instead of piddling around here with some old car?"

Riley stopped a few feet away, planted his feet, and crossed his arms. "So. You gonna keep brooding back here like some kind of tragic country song, or you actually gonna do something?"

Acen didn't answer. He just stared at the sun-drenched horizon past the tree line, jaw clenched tight enough to ache.

Riley tilted his head. "You should've told her the truth back then."

Acen finally turned to look at him, eyes narrowed. "What good would that have done? It wouldn't have changed anything."

"Maybe not," Riley said evenly. "But it would've mattered. To her. Hell, it would've mattered to *me*. You left us all in the dark."

Acen blew out a slow breath. "I didn't know how. Everything was a mess. I figured the cleanest thing I could do was walk away."

"Well, congratulations," Riley said, spreading his hands. "You did just that. Clean break and all. And now she's out there having dinner with Mr. Perfect Hair last night while you're stomping holes out here in gravel this morning."

The sound of a lawnmower fired up in the distance, and a blue jay squawked noisily from the edge of the roof before taking off across the open lot. The sun beat down heavier now, casting harsh shadows across the edge of the garage and making the asphalt out front shimmer like a stovetop.

Acen scrubbed his hand down his face. "It wasn't just Briana. It was everything. My folks. My plans. Me not being good enough."

"You're telling *me* that *now*?" Riley shook his head, incredulous. "Man, if you'd said that to Rose twenty years ago, she might've understood. She might've even fought for you."

Acen looked away, shame simmering low in his chest. "She deserved better."

"Maybe. But she wanted *you*, back then. And all she got was silence." He crossed his arms. "And I was too much of a coward to call you out on it all these years. I wanted to keep your friendship more than I wanted the truth for my sister. I'm no saint myself."

A heavy pause settled between them, thick as the Tennessee humidity. The kind of silence that said neither of them really had the words to patch old wounds. Not completely.

Finally, Riley stepped closer, lowering his voice. "You think Rose is the kind of woman you can wait on forever? She's been standin' on her own two feet for two decades. Built a life. Built a *business*. Built a damn softball team. All without you."

"I know."

"If you want her back, you're gonna have to give her something real this time. Not half-truths and long looks from across the room."

Acen stared down at the gravel, where his boots had worn a shallow groove. "I don't even know if she wants me."

"Well," Riley said, clapping a hand on his shoulder, "there's one sure way to find out."

Acen didn't move.

Riley stepped back and gestured toward the lot, where the clatter of tools and voices floated from the open garage bay. "Better do it soon, brother. Before that shiny new boy with the button-down charm makes her forget you ever existed."

A truck rumbled by on the main road, radio blaring something twangy about second chances and broken hearts. Acen barely heard it. His mind was full of Rose

—how she'd looked in the golden light outside The Silver Catfish, hair falling loose around her shoulders. The way her eyes had softened when she laughed with Declan. How easy it looked.

Too easy.

He wasn't ready to give up. Not yet.

But easy? No. Nothing about Rose had *ever* been easy. And she was worth every damn mile of the uphill road.

He looked up, toward the tree line and the distant shimmer of the lake. Somewhere in that direction was a woman who used to know his every fault—and loved him anyway, for a while.

Maybe it wasn't too late.

He straightened his shoulders and took a breath. Gravel crunched as he turned toward the front of the garage, boots scuffing the edge of his self-made path.

"Where you going?" Riley called after him.

Acen glanced back over his shoulder, something new in his eyes. "I've got a plan."

And just like that, he was gone—striding out from behind the garage into the heat and light of the morning, a man finally ready to tell the whole truth. Even if it meant standing in front of the fire.

Because when it came to Rose McAllister, half-measures just didn't cut it anymore.

CHAPTER ELEVEN

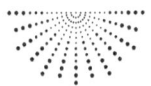

That afternoon, Rose stepped onto her porch, coffee in hand, planning to strategize for the upcoming playoffs and pretend the town hadn't exploded around her love life. She'd left Cindy running the coffee shop. Her thoughts too tangled and her face too much at the forefront of gossip for her taste.

Home was where she could slow down and think.

The mug was warm against her palms, the chipped ceramic familiar from years of use. She eased into her favorite rocker, the one that had belonged to her grandmother, and let the creak of its old joints settle into the rhythm of the cicadas. The lake glimmered down the hill, the surface broken now and then by a fish jumping or the breeze teasing across it. Ordinarily, this view would calm her, ground her, remind her why she'd stayed when others had left.

Today, though, her chest felt tight, and the coffee tasted bitter despite the three spoonsful of sugar she'd stirred in.

She'd told herself she'd focus on the tournament, map out lineups, run through batting rotations, and maybe draft a practice plan that would keep the women sharp without burning them out. Baseball strategy had always been her safe place—angles, averages, instincts she trusted more than her own heart.

But before she could settle into that comfort, her gaze snagged on something out of place.

A small wooden box sat on her porch swing.

Her steps slowed, every nerve in her body going taut. She hadn't heard a car pull up, hadn't seen anyone walking up the gravel drive. The box was plain golden oak wood, smoothed from age, no markings on the outside. Just... waiting.

Cautious, she set her coffee aside and crossed to it, her bare feet whispering against the planks. She half expected the thing to vanish when she blinked, like something conjured out of her restless thoughts. But it remained, squat and solid, the afternoon sun warming its edges.

Her hand hovered over the lid before she finally flipped it open.

Inside was a faded Polaroid.

Her breath caught.

The three of them - her, Riley, and Acen - stood in front of the lake, dripping wet from a swim, all gangly limbs and crooked smiles. She remembered the day instantly: late July, the heat sweltering, Riley daring her to jump from the dock even though the water was shallow there. Acen had ended up hauling them both out when their laughter left them gasping more than swimming.

She hadn't seen this photo in years.

The colors were time-bleached now, the whites yellowing, but the emotion was sharp as ever. Riley's hair stuck up at odd angles, his grin devilish. She looked carefree, flushed, younger than she'd thought herself even back then. And Acen - Lord help her - Acen stood between them with his arm draped across their shoulders like it had always belonged there.

Beneath the photo lay a folded piece of paper.

She hesitated, then smoothed it open.

Scrawled in dark ink was one line:

I never forgot. Not for a single day. −A

Her heart twisted. Her hand closed over the box as though to crush it.

And all the simple answers she'd been clinging to dissolved like sugar in sweet tea.

THE POLAROID SAT ON ROSE'S KITCHEN TABLE LIKE A ghost that refused to leave.

She'd carried it inside, set it down, and tried - Lord knows she'd tried - to ignore it. She'd even busied herself with chores: rinsing the coffee mug, sweeping the porch, folding the laundry piled on the couch. But no matter how many times she walked past the table, her eyes landed on that picture.

She'd studied it a dozen times already - the way her hair clung to her neck, how Riley squinted against the sun, Acen's arm casually slung around both their shoulders. That summer, they'd been inseparable. A trio made of secrets, loyalty, and the kind of laughter that echoed for days.

Back when everything was still simple. Before Briana. Before the goodbye that wrecked her.

The scrawled note was still in her hand. *I never forgot. Not for a single day.*

She wanted to hate it. To throw it out and claim the past was a closed door. She even moved toward the trash can once, her fingers gripping the paper so tightly the edges dug into her skin. But when she hovered over the open trash can, her fingers wouldn't cooperate. Would let the piece of paper, the piece of the past, drift away into oblivion.

Instead, she'd found herself sitting again, tracing the edges of the photograph with trembling fingers.

She didn't know what made her angrier - that Acen had kept something like this all these years - or that some small, foolish part of her heart still ached at the thought of him remembering.

The kitchen clock ticked, steady as a heartbeat.

Rose leaned back in her chair, arms folded tight across her chest. Outside, the afternoon shifted toward evening, shadows stretching long across the yard. Somewhere in the distance, kids shouted and laughed, their voices high and eager. The sound pulled at her, bittersweet.

She tried to focus on something else. Something that meant the world to her.

Baseball. Always baseball. It had been her refuge, her rhythm, the one place she could pour her hurt without it spilling over. Coaching her team, drilling the women on cutoffs and double plays, arguing over safe calls at second—it had kept her sane.

And Acen had to go and wedge himself right into the middle of it. Even baseball couldn't get her away from him now.

She could still see him on the field earlier that week, leaning against the fence line like he owned the place. Even injured, even out of the game, he carried himself with that same quiet confidence. The way his eyes tracked her when she pitched warmups had unsettled her more than she cared to admit.

Now this.

This box. This note.

A memory pressed into her palm like a bruise.

She picked up the Polaroid again, holding it at arm's length as though distance might dull its sting.

She remembered the moment it had been taken. Riley had stolen their mama's camera and insisted they commemorate their "last summer before adulthood." He'd called it their golden season. Rose had rolled her eyes at his dramatics, but she'd secretly agreed. That summer had been golden—sticky nights, bonfires, boat rides across Pickwick Lake, hours spent tossing a ball until their arms ached.

And Acen. Always Acen.

He'd been the center of it, though she'd never admitted it then. He made everything feel sharper, brighter. He challenged her in ways no one else dared —teasing her about her batting stance, racing her down the dock, kissing her in the shadows where Riley wouldn't see.

Her thumb brushed his image in the photo, her throat tightening.

She could almost feel the heat of his arm slung across her shoulders, smell the lake water drying on his skin. She remembered how her heart had pounded that day, not from the swim but from standing so close to him, wondering if he'd lean down and steal another kiss.

Instead, he'd just grinned for the camera, easy as breathing.

And then he'd left.

Rose pressed the heel of her hand to her eyes, trying to steady herself.

It had been twenty years. Twenty years of silence, of anger, of rebuilding a life brick by brick without him. She'd told herself she was over it, that the girl she'd been back then had grown into a woman who knew better than to pine after someone who'd walked away.

And for the most part, she believed it.

But the note cracked something in her she hadn't expected. *I never forgot. Not for a single day.*

Why send it now? Why dig up what was buried?

She thought of Acen's face when she'd seen him again, the shadows under his eyes, the way he'd stood like a man carrying more weight than he knew how to set down. She thought of the limp in his gait, the hint of pain he'd tried to hide.

She hated that part of her wanted to believe the note. That he hadn't forgotten. That she hadn't been erased.

Her hand tightened on the paper.

Because if he remembered… then maybe she wasn't crazy for remembering too.

The air in the kitchen felt too close. Rose shoved back from the table and moved to the back door, stepping onto the porch. The sun was dropping low, bleeding gold and pink across the lake. Fireflies sparked in the hedges, winking like tiny lanterns.

She drew in a breath, steadying herself. She'd faced tougher things than an old photograph. She'd stood on the mound with a full count, bases loaded, knowing her team was counting on her. She'd endured gossip, heartbreak, her mama's illness after her daddy's death. She wasn't about to let Acen Wheeler undo her with a Polaroid.

Still, she carried the box back outside, setting it on

the porch rail. The wood gleamed in the last light of day, simple and unassuming.

But Rose knew better.

It wasn't just a box.

It was a match struck over old kindling.

And she wasn't sure whether to stomp it out... or let it burn.

CHAPTER TWELVE

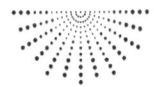

Acen parked at the far edge of the gravel lot that wrapped around the old softball field, cutting the engine before he reached the light poles. The sun was melting into a late-summer haze, streaking the sky with lavender and gold. A faint breeze stirred the smell of cut grass and clay, heavy with the familiar tang of dirt and sweat. The chorus of cicadas hummed like background music, rising and falling with the rhythm of the evening.

From where he sat in the shadow of his truck, he could see everything. The women's team was already spread across the diamond, warming up for practice. Dirty neon yellow softballs flashed against the deepening dusk, flying from glove to glove. Cleats scraped across the infield, sending up soft puffs of red dust. Laughter carried on the breeze, mixed with shouted calls to "Tag up!" and "Nice catch!"

And then there was Rose.

She stood near the dugout, clipboard in hand like it was an extension of her arm, barking directions with the kind of authority that only came from years of being listened to. Her auburn hair was pulled back into a messy knot at the base of her neck, loose strands catching the fading light like copper threads. She wore an old team T-shirt, faded from countless washes, tucked into shorts that showed the powerful lines of her legs shaped by hours of running bases and drilling line drives.

She looked… steady.

Like she belonged exactly where she was, with her team circling around her, with her feet planted in the dirt of this field, with that clipboard like a shield and a banner both.

She looked like home.

Acen gripped the steering wheel tighter, trying to summon the courage to move. He'd told himself all day that this was the right thing, that honesty was overdue. But watching her now, so rooted, so sure of herself and her place in the world, it was like his feet weighed twice what they should.

Still, he forced himself out of the truck. Gravel crunched under his sneakers, announcing his presence before his voice did.

"Hey, Coach," he called.

Half the team turned in unison, like prairie dogs poking their heads up at the same sound. A ripple of recognition spread, accompanied by a few poorly hidden smirks.

And then Rose turned.

Her expression didn't falter, but her dark blue eyes did sharpen, and for a long beat, she simply stared at him. She didn't turn away, though, and that was something.

Acen walked slowly, careful not to kick up too much dust, careful not to look like he was in a hurry. He stopped just short of the dugout, where the chain-link fence rattled with the vibrations of girls tossing bats against the bench.

"Did you get the box?" he asked quietly.

"I did." Her arms crossed immediately, clipboard tucked under one elbow like she needed the barrier. "Interesting choice, showing up like a ghost and leaving breadcrumbs."

His mouth twitched, not quite a smile. "I didn't know what else to do."

"You could've just talked to me."

"I figured you didn't want to hear it."

"Then why now?" she shot back.

The team went on moving around them, but Acen felt the weight of half a dozen pairs of ears leaning in, pretending not to eavesdrop. Someone cracked a bat against the cage, the hollow ring reverberating like punctuation between them.

They stood silently until the team moved away from them.

Then, he shoved his hands deep in his pockets, shoulders hunched. "Because seeing you with him—Declan—it made me realize I've wasted enough time. I hurt you. I should've stayed. Or at least told you the truth."

Her eyes narrowed. "What truth?"

He hesitated. The cicadas droned louder, like they were filling in the silence he almost couldn't bear to break. He looked down at his sneakers, scuffed white with chalk dust, then back up at her.

"That Briana came to me," he said finally. "She told me Riley didn't approve of us being together. That he'd asked her to warn me off. She said if I was really Riley's friend, I'd leave you alone."

Rose blinked, incredulous. "That's ridiculous. Riley never said—"

"I know that now," Acen cut in, voice rough. "But I was eighteen. Scared. Stupid. And then Briana kissed me and you saw it, and I didn't chase you down. I let it all fall apart."

Her voice was sharp as the crack of a bat. "You left."

"I thought I was protecting you. From the fallout. From my fears. From everything."

For a moment, all that moved was the bright neon yellow of a softball arching against the darkening sky. Rose stood still, clipboard tight against her chest, her jaw flexing.

"You were the one person who wasn't supposed to run," she said finally, softer this time.

Acen swallowed hard, throat dry. "I know. And I've regretted it every single day."

Something flickered across her face then—pain, recognition, maybe both. She let her arms drop slightly, not open, but not quite closed anymore either.

"It wasn't just a high school crush, Acen," she said, and her voice cracked in a way that nearly undid him. "I loved you."

He took a step closer before he realized he'd moved. "I loved you too."

"Then why didn't you fight for me?" Her question cut through the humid air like a fastball straight down the line.

His reply was barely more than a whisper. "Because I didn't think I was worth fighting for."

The words hung there, suspended between them like a ball waiting to drop.

Neither moved.

Around them, practice went on. A pop fly soared toward right field, and Ginny shouted for Dani to hustle. Tasha barked instructions from behind home plate. The clatter of bats echoed from the dugout. Life went on, ordinary and oblivious, while the ground between Rose and Acen cracked open.

Finally, Rose stepped back. Her face was unreadable again, shutters closed tight. "I don't know what you want from me."

"I don't want anything," Acen said quietly. "I just

needed you to know. What you do with it… that's up to you."

She nodded once, brisk, like she was calling a play. "I know you understand when I say I would prefer you not coach this practice. I need some space." Then she turned, her voice rising with practiced authority: "Dani, you're pitching today. Tasha's catching. Let's move."

And that was it.

She didn't look back.

Acen stood rooted in the dirt, watching her stride toward the field, clipboard already tapping against her thigh as she barked orders. She wasn't angry. She wasn't crying. She was steady.

That might've hurt worst of all.

He didn't know if he'd made things better or worse.

But at least now, the silence between them wasn't filled with lies.

It was filled with truth.

And maybe, just maybe, that was a start.

CHAPTER THIRTEEN

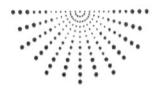

Rose didn't sleep.

She lay flat on her back, sheets twisted at her ankles, the ceiling fan above spinning in the highest setting making crazy circles like it was mocking her restlessness. The night air felt thick as molasses, June heat clinging stubborn even with the windows cracked open. Every cicada in Pickwick Bend seemed to have joined in a chorus outside her window, buzzing loud enough to make her teeth ache.

But it wasn't the noise keeping her up.

It was his words.

I didn't think I was worth fighting for.

The sentence kept looping through her chest, an ache that settled deep, like a bruise she hadn't noticed until someone pressed on it. She hated how it still hurt. Hated more that it still mattered.

Around two, she rolled over, hugging her pillow,

but her body felt electric, restless, like her skin didn't fit right. At three, she sat up, stared at the sliver of moonlight spilling across the hardwood floor, and considered calling him just to scream. By four, she gave up, shoved the pillow aside, and sat in the quiet darkness, knees pulled up, head in her hands.

When dawn finally bled pink streamers across the sky, she was raw from exhaustion. Her eyes burned, her head pounded, and her heart felt split clean in two.

By the time the sun crested over the trees, she needed air. She didn't even wait for the coffee pot to sputter. She slipped into running shorts and a T-shirt, shoved her tangled hair under a ballcap, grabbed her keys, and let her truck rattle down the winding backroad that curved through pines and maples.

The one place she knew she'd get the truth, plain and sharp as a nail, was at Aunt Jean's. A great aunt on her daddy's side. A Campbell by birth and a McAlister by marriage. A woman who believed in speaking the truth no matter that it might hurt in the telling. Herself or anyone else. Not an easy woman to live with, but one to have your back always if she loved you.

Jean's shotgun house sat on the far side of town, painted sunflower yellow like she dared the sun itself to outshine her. The porch sagged a little in the middle, but it was covered in pots of herbs, brightly colored clay gnomes, and wild morning glories twisting up the railing like they owned the place. Wind chimes dangled everywhere—copper, glass, seashells—and together they clattered and sang, sounding like ghosts arguing in a storm.

Jean was eighty if she was a day, but still strong enough to haul her own firewood, mow her own grass, and whip any man at cards. She had skin like creased parchment, eyes sharp as broken glass, and a voice that could hush a room full of rowdy men at the Moose Lodge.

Jean opened the door before Rose could knock, apron still tied around her waist. "You look like you've been up all night makin' bad decisions."

Rose tried for a smile, but it faltered.

Jean didn't press. Just stepped aside and waved her in. "Come on. Coffee's hot."

Inside, the little shotgun house smelled like chicory coffee, fried bacon, and the faint medicinal bite of salve Jean kept for her knees. Every surface was crowded—family photos in frames, jars of dried herbs, stacks of church bulletins. It was chaos, but the kind of chaos that felt lived in, not messy.

Jean poured coffee into mismatched mugs, shoved a honey biscuit across the table, and sat herself down. "Talk."

Rose didn't sugarcoat it. She told her everything - about Declan showing up shiny as a new penny, about the dinner that felt too easy, about the wooden box on her porch with the Polaroid and the note that cracked her chest open, about Acen's confession on the ball field.

She spilled it all while Jean sipped her coffee steadily, not blinking, not interrupting, just listening like she was collecting puzzle pieces she already knew the shape of.

When Rose finally stopped, her throat dry and her chest hollow, Jean leaned back, crossed her wiry arms, and said flat as stone: "You're mad he left."

"Yes."

Jean didn't soften. She never did. "Here's the thing about old wounds, Rosie girl. They don't stop bleedin' just because you slap a smile on 'em. You gotta clean 'em out. You gotta dig down to the bone sometimes."

Rose blinked. "And what if I dig and all I find is more pain?"

Jean's sharp eyes went soft. "Then you know you cared enough for it to hurt. That's not weakness. That's love."

The words settled heavy between them. Rose stared at the honey biscuit she hadn't touched. Her stomach was tied up too tight to eat.

"But what about Declan?" she asked finally, voice small.

Jean grinned and leaned forward. "Declan's a damn fine biscuit. Golden, warm, probably good for you. But Acen?" She tapped her finger on the table. "He's the one who burned your tongue when you were too eager to bite."

Rose groaned, burying her face in her hands. "Why do you always talk in metaphors?"

Jean snorted. "Because you're a McAllister. Y'all don't listen unless it sounds poetic."

Rose laughed despite herself, tears stinging the corners of her eyes. She swiped them away quickly, embarrassed at how close to breaking she felt. "You think I should forgive him?"

"I think," Jean said, leveling her gaze, "you ought to decide whether you're still in love with him. And if you are - stop pretendin' you're not. That's just foolish."

The silence that followed wasn't empty. It hummed with all the things Rose wanted to say but couldn't.

She thought of Declan's easy smile, the way he showed up without shadows trailing him. A man who offered stability, maybe even a future without complication.

Then she thought of Acen. The ache of him. The way just standing near him felt like stepping into sunlight and fire all at once. The man who'd broken her heart - but who'd also been the first person she ever truly gave it to.

Her throat tightened. "What if I choose wrong?"

Jean reached across the table, her weathered hand covering Rose's. "Then you'll survive. Just like I did when your uncle Earl ran off with that hair stylist from Corinth. Thought my world ended. It didn't. It cracked wide open, and I built somethin' new."

Rose blinked. "You never told me that story."

Jean smirked. "Because it wasn't about him. It was about me."

The wind outside shifted, rattling the chimes like laughter and warning all at once. Rose let the sound fill the silence.

Finally, Jean gave her hand a squeeze. "Stop runnin' from the hurt, Rosie girl. It'll follow you no matter where you go. The only way through it is to stand still and face it."

Rose nodded, though the lump in her throat made it hard to breathe.

Jean leaned back, finishing her coffee. "Now eat that biscuit before I box your ears. You look half-starved."

Rose laughed again, shaky but real this time, and picked it up.

The honey clung to her fingers, sticky and sweet, and as she bit into the warm, crumbly bread, she thought of Acen's note again. *I never forgot. Not for a single day.*

And she wondered, not for the first time, if maybe she hadn't either.

CHAPTER FOURTEEN

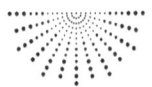

By the time Rose got to the field for Thursday night practice, the air was thick—summer heat mingling with something heavier. The June evening pressed close, sticky as molasses, and the cicadas had already struck up their ragged orchestra from the trees lining the outfield fence. The sky was still painted with late sunlight, streaks of pink and orange bleeding into blue, but the light had a tired quality, like even the heavens were worn out.

Her players were already warming up. Usually that meant laughter, easy banter, a few good-natured shoves as gloves popped and balls smacked leather. Tonight, though, the sound was subdued. Voices dropped lower, movements slowed, and eyes - too many of them - kept flicking between Rose and the outfield as though the girls were waiting for a storm to roll in.

Rose chalked it up to gossip fatigue. The town had been buzzing all week, her name bouncing around diner booths and church foyers like a pinball nobody could stop. Apparently, every waitress and cousin-twice-removed had a hot opinion on who Rose McAllister ought to love, forgive, or kick to the curb. She wasn't sure if she wanted to laugh or scream about it.

Glancing around the field, she didn't see Acen. Relief washed through her, quick and guilty. Good. He was giving her time, the space she'd asked for without ever saying it out loud. The truth he'd dropped in her lap on Tuesday had been heavy enough to bruise. She still felt the ache of it, like she'd been carrying a weighted bat around since the moment he said it: *I didn't think I was worth fighting for.*

And Lord help her, she hadn't been able to stop thinking about it.

But town gossip and news she hadn't wanted to hear couldn't be allowed to interfere with their regional championship. She'd talk to Acen tomorrow. Tell him she wanted to shelve any conversation about the two of them until after the tournament season. She had her pride. Lord knew that at times that pride had been the only thing that kept her going over the years, but the team could use his extra edge and experience to put them over the top and get the trophy this year. She just had to figure out a way to keep all the other distractions out of her mind until then.

She blew out a breath and forced her focus to the field. Clipboard tucked under her arm; she started setting up the batting drills. Routine helped. Toss balls in the bucket. Chalk a new line in the dirt. Straighten the net. Remind Tasha she needed to keep her knees bent. All the little pieces that made sense when nothing else did.

She was halfway through when Dani jogged over. The girl's ponytail bounced like it was wired, nervous energy practically sparking off her. Her glove was tucked under one arm, but she fidgeted with the strap as if she couldn't decide whether to hold it or drop it.

"You okay?" Rose asked, keeping her voice calm.

Dani bit her lip. "Um. That depends."

"On what?"

"On how mad you're gonna be that I didn't warn you sooner."

Rose's eyes narrowed, clipboard shifting against her chest. "Warn me about—?"

"Hey, stranger."

The voice came from behind her.

Rose froze. Her breath stopped short, the air in her lungs turned thick as syrup. That voice hadn't changed in twenty years. Smoky. Sweet. Practiced, the kind of tone meant to disarm, to charm, to cover sharp edges.

Slowly, because she already knew, Rose turned.

There stood Briana Lewis.

Time hadn't softened her. If anything, it had carved her sharper. Her honey-blonde hair, once teased and sprayed into whatever style was in vogue at Pickwick High, was now tucked neatly under a designer ball cap that absolutely did not belong at a rec-league practice. Her jeans hugged too tight, her top looked catalog-fresh, and her sneakers were white in a way no shoes worn to a dusty field had any right to be. She didn't fit the setting, but Briana had always been like that—like she was auditioning for some life just out of reach.

Her smile, though, was the same. Tight as a fishing line right before it snapped.

"What are you doing here?" Rose asked, voice flat.

"I heard you were coaching." Briana swept a hand toward the girls on the field. "Thought I'd swing by, see the legendary Pickwick Pirate Queens in action."

Rose stared at her. "And you just happened to be back in town after two decades?"

"Property stuff, remote job, kind of a break to reset my life." Briana gave a casual shrug, too studied to be natural. "My dad left me the old Lewis place. Figured I'd check in, clean it out, maybe fix it up."

Rose crossed her arms, the clipboard pressed to her ribs like armor. "And of all the places you could 'check in,' you landed here?"

Briana's smile faltered. Just a flicker, but Rose caught it. "Look, Rose. I know we didn't part on the best of terms."

"You mean when you made out with my boyfriend behind the gym and told him my brother didn't want him to be with me?"

Gasps rippled from the players who'd been eaves-dropping, though none of them looked surprised. Pickwick loved its old stories, and this one had been whispered like scripture over a lot of years.

Briana's cheeks flushed, but she lifted her chin. "That was high school."

"And you were a traitor," Rose shot back. Her throat was tight, but her voice was steady. "That wasn't teenage drama, Bree. That was betrayal."

The field went still. Gloves hung loose. Softballs rolled to a stop. Even the cicadas seemed to pause, like the whole world was listening.

"I didn't come here to fight," Briana said finally, her voice softer now, stripped of its practiced lilt. "I came to say I'm sorry."

Rose blinked, stunned. "You waited twenty years to apologize?"

Briana swallowed. "I thought you hated me."

"I did."

"Do you still?"

Rose opened her mouth. Closed it again. The truth was slippery. Anger still simmered under her ribs, but so did exhaustion, and grief, and maybe—just maybe—a strange sense of relief hearing Briana finally say the words.

"I don't know what I feel," Rose admitted. "But I don't need you showing up here like we're gonna braid each other's hair and share a lemonade. This team?

These girls? They're my family now. You don't get to drop back in and stir things up."

Briana nodded, and for once, she didn't smile. "Fair enough. I just wanted to say it. I'm sorry."

Without waiting for a reply, she turned. Her footsteps were slow, but steady, crunching over gravel and grass as she walked back toward the parking lot. Her posture was straight, like she wasn't used to hearing no.

Rose didn't move. Didn't speak. She just stood there, clipboard clutched too tight, heart thudding so hard she could feel it in her wrists. The sun slid lower, bleeding red into the horizon, and her past slinked off into the shadows again.

PRACTICE ENDED EARLY.

No one could focus after that. Drills turned sloppy, balls sailed wild, and Rose had snapped—almost without meaning to—at Tasha for dropping an easy catch. The girl's face had crumpled, and Rose had swallowed her temper down like vinegar. She waved them off after only an hour, muttering something about the heat.

The second the last cleat cleared the field, Rose sank onto the bleachers. The metal was still warm from the sun, and she let her elbows rest on her knees, head dropping into her hands. She felt wrung out, scraped raw by ghosts she hadn't asked to face.

"Need backup?"

The voice was familiar.

Riley dropped a cold soda beside her and lowered himself onto the bench with the ease of someone who'd been sitting beside her all their lives. He cracked his own can open, the fizz loud in the humid air.

"Do you ever mind your business?" she muttered without looking up.

"Nope. Not when it comes to my sister." He took a long swallow. "So. Briana?"

"She just showed up." Rose lifted her head, brushing a stray hair from her face. "Like we're gonna hug it out and pretend nothing happened."

"She always had nerve," Riley said dryly.

Rose snorted. "That's one way to put it." Her gaze drifted back to the field, the bases still gleaming faintly white in the dusk. "She said she's sorry."

Riley was quiet for a long beat, the kind of silence only siblings could share without discomfort. Then: "Do you believe her?"

"I don't know." Rose wrapped her hands around the soda can but didn't open it. "I don't even know if it matters."

"It might," Riley said. His tone was even, but his eyes, sharp and steady, gave away more. "Especially if she's not just back for the reasons she's spreading around town."

Rose frowned, turning toward him. "What's that supposed to mean?"

He didn't answer right away. Instead, he leaned back, stretched his legs out, and took another sip like he had all the time in the world. But his gaze wasn't on her anymore.

It had drifted toward the parking lot.

Rose followed it.

And there, just visible behind a clump of trees, sat Acen's truck. Quiet. Shadowed. Watching.

Her breath caught.

Suddenly, she wasn't so sure she'd survived the past after all.

CHAPTER FIFTEEN

Rose didn't go home after practice.

Instead, she drove.

No destination, no plan—just the steady hum of the road beneath her tires and the gnawing wildfire in her chest that refused to quiet. She kept the windows cracked, the humid night air spilling in like a second heartbeat, sticky and insistent. The dashboard clock glowed, ticking away minutes she couldn't account for. Every turn of the steering wheel felt both aimless and necessary, like if she just kept moving long enough, the heat inside her might burn itself out.

But of course, it wasn't just heat. It was Briana.

Only Briana could still rattle her this way after twenty years.

Rose hated that truth with every mile marker she passed.

It wasn't just the surprise of seeing her again—it

was the memory Briana unearthed simply by existing. That ache of betrayal that had never fully scabbed over. And beneath all of it was something worse: that ugly, dangerous whisper of *what if*.

What if things could've been different if they'd all just told the truth back then?

What if Acen had fought for her instead of walking away?

What if Briana hadn't lied to her face, hadn't stolen something she could never give back?

What if Rose herself had dared to ask why instead of letting her pride close the door?

The road stretched on, lined with trees and fields that shimmered in the dusky light. Her headlights caught flashes of old barns, broken fences, a deer darting across the ditch. The familiar landmarks blurred together until she couldn't tell if she was circling Pickwick or circling herself.

By the time she finally parked, she realized her hands had carried her somewhere her heart knew better than her head. The lake.

Pickwick Lake lay sprawled before her, dark and gleaming under the bruised sky. The water reflected the last shreds of daylight like broken glass, violet and copper streaks caught on a restless surface. The dam a black silhouette against the colors. She slid out of the truck and perched on the hood, her bare feet dangling, the metal warm beneath her.

The air smelled of fish and honeysuckle, with an

undercurrent of damp earth that reminded her of summers spent sneaking out past curfew. Out here, cicadas sang their endless chorus, and the world felt both infinite and crushingly small.

Rose tipped her head back, staring at the sky deepening into indigo. Maybe she needed to stop running from the ghosts that haunted her. The Polaroid. The note. Briana's voice like a blade disguised as honey. Acen's eyes that still had the power to make her heart stutter.

Maybe it was time to face them.

She didn't know how long she sat there before the moon rose, a pale coin climbing slow and steady, casting the lake in silver. She shivered, though the night was warm, then slid off the hood and drove home before she could change her mind.

LATER, SHE SAT ON HER PORCH, WRAPPED IN A SILK shawl that had belonged to her mother, holding a mug of tea she hadn't touched. The steam had long since faded, but the weight of the ceramic felt like something to cling to. The porch light glowed soft around her, moths batting themselves senseless against it, while the crickets carried on below.

Her thoughts wouldn't settle. They circled like crows, loud and insistent, landing and taking flight again.

So, when headlights flared at the end of her driveway, she wasn't surprised.

Of course. Because this day couldn't end without one more ghost showing up.

Acen's truck rolled to a slow stop. The engine idled a moment before going quiet, and the night seemed to lean in. He didn't move right away, and neither did she. They sat suspended in that charged silence, as if both of them were waiting for the other to blink first.

Finally, he climbed out and walked toward the porch, his boots crunching over gravel. He stopped at the steps, not daring further without permission. The porch light caught the lines on his face, the wear of years she hadn't seen, but the shadow in his eyes was the same.

"She came to practice," Rose said before he could speak. "Briana."

"I know." His voice was low. "I saw her."

Her stomach twisted. He'd been there. Watching. Like a storm on the horizon, waiting.

"Must be nice," she said, bitterness leaking into her tone. "To have two women still hung up on you after all this time."

"I don't want two women, Rose." His answer was sharp, unhesitating. He shifted one step closer, as if pulled by some gravity he couldn't fight.

"I want *you*."

The words were simple. Too simple.

She met his eyes, her own tired but clear. "Then stop talking and start proving it."

She didn't invite him in. She didn't need the intimacy of shared walls and closed doors. Not tonight. She stayed wrapped in her shawl on the porch, the mug cooling against her palms, a fragile anchor to keep her steady.

Acen stayed two steps down, shoulders tense but eyes steady. He looked like a man braced for judgment, for either mercy or exile. And Rose—well, Rose decided to let him sweat.

"You can say you want me all day," she said finally. "But words are easy. I've heard enough of them to last a lifetime."

"I know."

"I don't need promises, Acen. I need truth. I need action."

He nodded, jaw working. "What do you want to know?"

Rose studied him. Really studied. Not the boy she'd fallen for at eighteen, not the ghost she'd hated for twenty years, but the man standing on her porch now. His hair darker, threaded with the faintest streaks of silver. His shoulders broader, marked by work and life. His eyes—the same, but older, too.

"Why did you leave like that?" she asked. The question scraped her throat raw. "That night—after Briana kissed you. You didn't call. You didn't write. You just vanished."

Acen rubbed the back of his neck, a nervous tic she remembered all too well. His voice came heavy.

"Because I was ashamed. Because I thought... you saw what happened and made up your mind. You turned and walked away, Rose, and I figured you were done with me. And I thought maybe you were right to be."

She swallowed, the lump in her throat thick. "You thought I should have fought harder?"

"No." His answer came quick, fierce. "I thought I should've. But I didn't. I froze. I took the coward's exit. And I've regretted it every damn day since."

Rose stared into her mug, at the tea she hadn't drunk, watching the faint ripples catch the porch light.

"I waited for you," she said, barely more than a whisper. "For a call. A letter. Anything. And when it never came, I made myself hate you. Because that was easier than wondering what I did wrong."

"You didn't do anything wrong," he said, voice low but certain. "You were the best thing I had, Rose. And I let my fear ruin it."

Her chest ached, a dull ache that carried twenty years of weight. But she didn't let it soften her. Not yet.

"I need to know," she said finally. "If this is real. If this is something you want. Not because it's familiar. Not because you're lonely. Not because we have history. But because you see me *now*. As I am."

Acen's gaze held hers, unflinching. "I do. And I want to show you. However long it takes."

The night pressed close, heavy with crickets and the occasional croak of a frog by the pond. Rose let out a slow breath, watching the condensation curl in the warm summer air.

"I need time, Acen. I wasn't expecting this. I wasn't expecting you to come swooping back into town and disrupt everything I've built." She pulled the blanket tighter around her shoulders despite the heat of the night air. "Can you give me that?"

"Yes." The word came steady. Solid.

She sighed, the sound carrying weariness and something else - maybe the faintest flicker of hope. "Okay." She sipped the lukewarm tea. "I still need you to help coach the team. I'm not so proud that I can let those ladies down after all their hard work because you and I have some issues to work out. They need the edge you can give them. So, this is what we're going to do. On the ballfield, we are just coaches. Nothing more. No personal stuff. Ever."

Acen nodded once. "I can do that."

And for the first time all night, she almost believed him.

"Good. I'll see you at the game. It's Madison County and they're tough as nails."

"I won't let you down." His eyes stared straight into her soul, implying much more than softball games was at stake.

She watched him get back into his truck and melt away into the night.

CHAPTER SIXTEEN

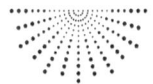

T he next morning, Rose walked into Southern
Sips prepared to take the day in stride. But
first, a cinnamon roll and some sanity.

A full breakfast at The Mimosa Tree would only
raise her stress level because the gossip mill was surely
in full swing, every forkful of biscuits and gravy punc-
tuated with someone whispering about Acen Wheeler's
reappearance, Briana's strut across the ball field, and
Rose McAllister caught dead center of it all.

Southern Sips was safer ground.

The coffee shop already hummed with the kind of
low-level chaos that made it feel alive. Mismatched
chairs scraping across hardwood, weekenders in golf
polos, locals leaning heavy on the counter like they
owned the place. The scent of cinnamon and strong
coffee clung to the air, tangling with laughter and

clinking mugs. The chalkboard menu listed quirky lattes with names like "Pickwick Perk" and "Lake Life Caramel."

Cindy, her hair piled high in a messy knot and apron dusted with flour, waved her over from behind the counter. "You look like someone who's about to ruin a man's life."

"Just his sense of security," Rose muttered, setting her sunglasses on top of her head.

"Oh good." Cindy grinned as she slid muffins onto a tray. "You're finally embracing your villain era."

Rose cracked a reluctant smile.

"Acen come by again?" Cindy asked, her tone casual but her eyes sharp, the way only a friend could pull off.

Rose nodded. "We talked. He didn't run."

"Progress," Cindy declared, stacking muffins high.

"I told him he had to show up. Prove he meant it."

Cindy arched a brow. "And Briana?"

Just as she'd feared, the ball field debacle had already made the rounds. Word traveled faster in Pickwick Bend than kudzu climbing a fencepost.

"She's sniffing around," Rose admitted. "Still polished. Still poisonous."

"Want me to dump sugar in her gas tank?"

"No," Rose said, though her lips twitched. "But maybe don't serve her the good coffee if she comes in."

Cindy winked. "Consider it done."

Rose slid her cinnamon roll onto a plate, grabbed her coffee, and made her way to the corner booth. The one with the cushion that sagged just enough to feel familiar.

She let her shoulders drop. She felt… lighter.

Not fixed. Not healed.

But maybe, just maybe, she wasn't walking through the wreckage alone anymore.

She tore into the cinnamon roll, the icing still warm, letting the sweetness steady her nerves. The chatter around her floated like background music. Mr. Landry griping about gas prices, two teenagers arguing over who'd pitched better in Little League last season, the sound of the espresso machine hissing like a sigh.

It almost felt normal.

Until the bell over the door jingled, and Rose glanced up to see Declan stroll in.

Her fork froze midair.

Declan looked like trouble packaged in charm that morning. Sun-browned skin, sleeves rolled up to his elbows, and that easy, confident smile that seemed to land right on her like he'd been saving it just for her. He spotted her instantly and cut through the crowd, a fresh energy rolling in with him like a gust of lake wind.

"Morning, McAllister," he said, sliding into the booth next to her without waiting for an invite. "Thought I'd find you hiding out here."

"Not hiding," she said, though her tone lacked conviction. "Strategically avoiding."

"Ah." He leaned back, grin lazy. "The art of small-town survival. I'm still learning."

She tried not to notice the way people's heads swiveled. Because of course they did. Declan was new enough to still be shiny, and sitting with Rose only poured gasoline on the rumor fire already blazing through town.

"You want half this cinnamon roll?" she asked, mostly to distract herself.

"Darlin', I came in for coffee, but if you're offering…" He reached over, tore off a piece, and popped it into his mouth like they'd been sharing breakfasts forever.

Rose forced a laugh, though something low in her stomach twisted. Because it wasn't lost on her what this looked like.

And apparently, it wasn't lost on Acen either.

Because when the bell jingled again, and she glanced up, there he was.

Acen froze just inside the door, scanning the coffee shop like a man bracing for a hit. His eyes on her corner booth, on her and Declan sitting shoulder to shoulder over half a cinnamon roll.

The muscle in his jaw ticked.

Rose's breath caught.

Acen didn't move for a long moment, and she swore the air shifted, heavy with unsaid words. Then, without a sound, he turned and headed for the counter, nodding stiffly to Cindy as if he hadn't seen a thing.

But Rose knew better.

Declan followed her gaze, his grin fading as he leaned closer. "That him?"

Rose cleared her throat. "Yep."

"Ah." Declan studied her a moment, then Acen's broad back at the counter. "Guess the stories aren't exaggerated."

Her heart kicked up. "What stories?"

"That you two have enough history to fill a library." His tone was teasing, but his eyes were careful. "Am I walking into a minefield here?"

She stared at him, fork still in hand, cinnamon icing smudged on her napkin, the whole coffee shop holding its collective breath like they were all waiting for her answer.

Maybe she was walking into a minefield too.

The rest of breakfast blurred around the edges, half conversation with Declan, half awareness of Acen at the counter. He didn't come over. Didn't even look her way again. He just grabbed his coffee, muttered thanks to Cindy, and walked out with that steady stride that screamed control—but Rose knew it for what it was.

Restraint.

And that almost hurt worse than if he'd made a scene.

Declan noticed too. "Man's got discipline," he said, shaking his head. "Not sure I'd have the same if the roles were reversed." His eyes smiled into hers. "I know you have your hands full with practices and the tournament and that's as it should be. But I want you to know I'd love to get together again soon."

Rose pressed her napkin flat against the table, her pulse unsteady. "You're right. I have a lot going on right now. It's complicated. Let's get past the tournament and circle back, okay?"

"Complicated," Declan repeated, then softened it with a smile. "That's just another way of saying interesting."

But she wasn't sure interesting was what she wanted anymore.

By the time she left Southern Sips, the sun was high and the heat oppressive, but the bigger weight was inside her. Declan had walked her out, his hand brushing lightly against her arm as he promised to see her at the game. It was easy with him. Comfortable. He liked her without ghosts.

But she couldn't shake the look on Acen's face—the flash of hurt, quickly buried.

It lingered, sharper than vinegar on her tongue.

That night, sitting on her porch with the cicadas screaming and the Polaroid still on her kitchen table, Rose tried to untangle it all.

Acen's note. His presence on the field. The past. The new promises.

Declan's smile. His ease. His ability to step right into her life without dredging up the past.

And her own heart, traitorous and torn, beating harder than it had in years.

She closed her eyes, the night air thick, the lake a dark mirror in the distance.

She wanted simple. She wanted safe. But she was a McAllister. She'd never been either.

CHAPTER SEVENTEEN

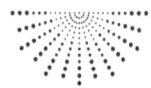

The next morning, Rose woke to the endless summer sound of cicadas humming outside her window and the faint smell of honeysuckle drifting in from the tree line.

She stretched, stood, and pulled her hair into a ponytail. Today wasn't about Declan, or Acen, or Briana, or ghosts that had been stirred from the past. Today was about her team. About the Pickwick Pirate Queens. If anything grounded her, it was those women. Laughing, sweating, hollering encouragement across the diamond.

Last practice before the first game of the tournament.

But first, a full day at Southern Sips.

As she unlocked the door, Sarah and her husband, James, pulled into the parking lot. She waited for them to exit their car and walk onto the porch of the café.

"Good morning, y'all. What brings the two of you out so early? And during the week."

Sarah laughed as they came through the door. "We are officially retired and moving to Pickwick Bend full time."

"Congratulations! How about free coffee and muffins to celebrate your new status as locals?" Rose asked as she slipped behind the counter and started making coffee.

Once she had them settled with coffee and muffins, the day seemed to take off and rush by. Unusual for a weekday, but welcome as it made the day pass more quickly. The smiles and conversation with friends and strangers alike made for a good feeling. Southern Sips had been her brainchild, and its success meant the world to her.

Cindy burst through the door at four o'clock breathless.

"Sorry! I thought I might be late and didn't want to hold you up from getting to the ballfield." She panted.

"No worries." Rose said, taking off her logo apron and exiting the space behind the counter. "You're right on time."

"Good luck." Cindy called as the door shut behind her.

By the time she rolled into the gravel lot at the park, the sun had already baked the field into a haze of heat. Dust hung in the air, stirred up by cleats digging in the dirt by her team. The crack of a bat echoed sharp, followed by a round of groans and whoops from the little league field adjacent to their own.

Then, she saw him. Acen. Leaning against the chain-link fence of their assigned field, glove in one hand, a bucket of balls at his feet. He was waiting. And just like he'd promised, he didn't try to cross that invisible line between them.

"Afternoon, Coach," he called, voice easy, steady.

The little scene in her coffee shop might never have happened. Rose gave him a curt nod, then turned her attention to the women jogging laps. "Let's pick it up, ladies! Tournament starts this Saturday, and we're gonna stomp some teams this year."

The chatter rose. Dani whooped, Ginny muttered something about melting in the sun, and Tasha yelled back, "Ain't no excuses, let's go!"

For a little while, it almost felt normal.

But normal had a way of slipping.

Because the second Briana Lewis showed up again, leaning against the bleachers in another one of her too-crisp outfits, sunglasses glinting, the atmosphere changed.

Rose caught the way half the team glanced toward her, then toward Acen, then back to Briana. Whispered chatter rippled like wildfire.

Rose set her jaw. "Focus! Grounders, let's move!"

Acen didn't look Briana's way. Not once. He crouched low, glove ready, voice sharp as he barked encouragement. "Square up! That's it, Dani! Use your hips, Ginny, don't arm-swing!"

They both ignored Briana, and the others followed their lead. Pushing their limits. Practicing with their whole heart.

Rose gathered the women at home plate, sweat shining on their foreheads, laughter bubbling in their throats. "Y'all did good today," she said, letting her voice carry. "Real good. Keep playing like this, we'll give that Madison County team a run for their money."

The women cheered, some clapping each other on the back, others chugging water like it was liquid gold.

Rose stood at the edge of the dugout with her clipboard, pretending to jot down notes when really she was trying not to let her temper flare. Giving Briana a chance to slink away.

When she looked up, Briana was still there.

Still leaning on those bleachers like she had every right to waltz back into Pickwick Bend and act like she owned the place. Her sunglasses glinted with the last of the evening sun, her hair glossy, her smile sharp enough to cut.

The women noticed. Of course they did.

Ginny leaned close, dropping her voice low as she pretended to tie her shoe. "That's her, right?"

Rose didn't answer.

Dani, never one to whisper when hollering would do, asked outright, "Coach, that your Briana?"

"My Briana?" Rose barked, heat rising in her cheeks. "She's not my anything."

The dugout went quiet for a beat, until Tasha piped up with a grin, "Well, she sure isn't here to cheer for us. She looks like she took a wrong turn on her way to Memphis. That outfit isn't for a ball field for sure."

That broke the tension, sending a ripple of laughter through the women. Even so, the air was thick, like the whole town's gossip was pressing against the chain-link fence.

Acen hadn't said a word. He just kept raking the dirt around home plate, smoothing out the grooves where the women had dug in their cleats. His shoulders were tight, though, his jaw set. Rose could read him better than she cared to admit. He was holding back.

"Alright, ladies," Rose said, clapping her hands. "Before y'all go, we're running one more drill. Scrimmage. Half fielders, half batters. Let's see if we can pull it together under pressure."

Groans rose, but so did grins. Competition always lit a fire.

"Line up," Acen called, his voice carrying steady over the chatter.

The practice cracked to life—Tasha snagging a line drive with a little too much flair, Dani sliding into second like she thought ESPN might be watching, Ginny barking encouragement one second and complaining about the heat the next.

Rose's heart settled in its familiar rhythm. The sound of bat against ball, the smell of dust and leather, the laughter that followed every fumble.

But Briana didn't leave. She stayed, arms crossed, watching like she was studying a playbook only she knew.

And that burned.

Because Rose could feel her eyes. And she knew—just knew—that Briana was waiting for her to crack.

"Nice hustle!" Rose called, maybe a little louder than necessary, when Dani made it to third.

"Keep your elbow up, Ginny!" Acen hollered, his focus locked on the batter.

For a brief moment, Rose caught his gaze. He wasn't looking at Briana. He wasn't distracted. He was in it—with her, with the team. And Lord help her, that steadied something in her chest.

Still, when the scrimmage ended and the women collapsed in the dugout with water bottles and red cheeks, Briana finally made her move.

She sauntered down the bleachers, heels clicking against the metal, and stopped right at the edge of the field.

"Well," she said, her voice sugar-sweet but edged with steel. "This is cute. Y'all really do take this little hobby seriously."

The team stiffened.

Rose planted her clipboard on the bench, stood, and

walked forward. "It isn't a hobby. It's a team. And we work harder than you'd know."

"Oh, I know." Briana's smile didn't waver. "I was on a team once, remember? Back when summers meant something more than—what? Grown women sweating out here in the dirt?"

"That's enough," Acen said, stepping forward, his voice low but firm.

Briana's gaze flicked to him. "Oh, Acen. Always playing protector. Some things never change."

Rose's blood ran hot. "Why are you here, Briana?"

Briana tilted her head. "Maybe I missed home. Maybe I missed old friends." She let the pause hang, her eyes glinting. "Or maybe I just wanted to see how much dust could settle on the past before somebody finally stirred it back up."

Rose felt the team's eyes dart between them like it was a tennis match.

She wanted to scream, to demand answers, to drag every lie Briana had spun out into the open. But her women didn't need to see her unravel. Not here. Not on this field.

So she took a breath, steadied her voice, and said, "Practice is over. Y'all head on home."

The team hesitated, reluctant to leave the show, until Tasha clapped her hands. "C'mon, ladies. Let's clear out."

One by one, they filed past, throwing curious looks

over their shoulders, until it was just Rose, Acen, and Briana left on the diamond.

The cicadas were loud again. The sky was bleeding pink and gold. And Rose's chest felt like it might split.

"You had no right to show up here," she said finally.

"And you had no right to act like I don't exist," Briana shot back, her sweetness gone now. "We have history too, Rose. You don't get to erase that."

Rose stepped closer. "History doesn't mean I owe you anything. Not after what you pulled."

Briana's lips curved. "Still bitter after all these years. I almost admire it."

"Stop," Acen cut in, his voice rough. "This isn't the place—"

"Isn't it?" Briana turned to him, her eyes sharp. "You chose her then. You'll choose her now. And look how far that's gotten you—back in Pickwick Bend, chasing ghosts."

Acen didn't flinch. "I'm not chasing ghosts." He looked at Rose, steady. "I'm trying to make things right."

Rose's heart thudded.

For once, Briana looked caught off guard. Just for a flicker. Then she smiled, slow and knowing. "We'll see."

And with that, she turned and walked off, heels clicking against the gravel until the sound faded.

Silence pressed in.

Rose exhaled, long and shaky, and wrapped her arms around herself. "Well. That went about how I figured. And I sure didn't need her showing up and ruining the last practice before the game."

Acen stepped closer. "You okay?"

She gave a short laugh. "Define okay."

"Breathing. Standing. Still ready to fight."

She looked at him, tired and raw, but a smile tugged at her lips despite everything. "Guess I'm okay then."

"Don't let this rattle you. You and the team are ready to take the championship this year for sure."

They stood there, dusk thickening, fireflies beginning to spark at the edge of the outfield. The weight of the past was still there, heavy as ever. But, for now, it hovered in the background. Acen was right. She had this.

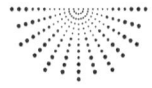

CHAPTER EIGHTEEN

S aturday morning dawned clear and hot, the kind of summer day that shimmered off asphalt and soaked through shirts before noon.

Game Day.

Rose arrived at the ballfield early, coffee in hand, hair pulled tightly back in her signature ponytail, clipboard tucked under her arm. The bleachers were still empty, but the smell of cut grass and concession stand popcorn lingered in the air like tradition. This field had seen heartbreak and home runs in equal measure. Today, it was about to see both.

The first game of the tournament season always carried the smell of gun powder and sweat and determination.

The Pickwick Pirate Queens were playing the Madison Marauders, their biggest rival and the team most likely to complain about Rose's "liberal interpretation" of the batting order.

She didn't care.

She was more focused on keeping her own team from imploding.

Because as much as she'd hoped practice would reset the mood, Briana's surprise appearance had shaken them all.

"Morning, Coach," Dani called, jogging up with her bat bag slung over one shoulder.

"Tell me you brought ibuprofen and optimism," Rose said.

"I brought a six-pack of both," Dani grinned. "We ready to beat the glitter off those Marauders?"

"Let's hope so."

One by one, the rest of the team trickled in—Tasha, with her game face on and hair braided like she was going to war. Ginny, all nerves and sunblock Maggie smacking gum like it was keeping words in her mouth she wanted to say but knew she shouldn't

By the time the opposing team arrived, the stands had started to fill.

And then Declan showed up.

Rose spotted him instantly - he stood out, even in a crowd. Gray T-shirt, jeans that hugged his frame too well, and a Pickwick Pirate Queen hat he'd found somewhere pulled low over his eyes. He picked a spot halfway up the bleachers, nodded to a few familiar faces, and sat down like he had every right to be there.

She hated how her stomach flipped. Hated how her heart picked up the beat just a little bit. Today was about the game. Not her love life. She waved casually when he looked in her direction, then put her thoughts firmly on the game and her strategy.

Then Briana arrived.

In a sundress. And wedges.

To a softball game.

"Of course she did," Rose muttered.

She ignored the looks and the low whisper of gossip that followed Briana's entrance. Instead, she turned her full focus to her team.

"All right, ladies," she said, gathering them in a tight circle near the dugout. "We play clean, we play smart, and we don't get rattled. No matter who's watching from the stands."

A few eyes darted to the bleachers.

Rose didn't flinch.

"You hear me?"

"Yes, Coach," came the chorus.

Acen arrived in the dugout and high-fived everyone.

"Alright, team. We've got this. Y'all know it. I know it. Let's show everyone in the stands what we've got."

A cheer loud enough to scare away a few birds that had perched on the roof of the dugout rang out drawing the attention of the fans who cheered right back.

Rose's spirits rose and she grinned at Acen.

The game started slow. Both teams tight, their bats quiet. By the third inning, it was still scoreless, and the sun was brutal.

But in the top of the fourth, something shifted.

Dani cracked a double down the third base line, and the dugout erupted. Tasha followed with a bloop single that brought her home. Suddenly, the Pickwick Pirate Queens were up by a run and the momentum turned.

Rose watched her team come alive—grinning, cheering, high-fiving like they were invincible.

And for a few glorious innings, it felt like the past couldn't touch her.

Until Briana sauntered down the bleachers and made a beeline for Acen who was sitting at the end of the dugout bench closest to the entrance. He was so focused on the game that he didn't even look up.

Rose's chest tightened.

She tried not to look.

But she couldn't not see the way Briana leaned in, all soft voice and tilted smile. Couldn't ignore the way Acen stiffened but didn't get up.

Couldn't stop the fear that maybe she was wrong to believe him.

Then he stood.

Not fast. Not dramatic.

But enough.

He stepped away from Briana. Said something quiet. Something final. And turned back to the game.

And Rose saw him choose *her*.

Without hesitation.

Briana didn't storm off. She simply pivoted, lips tight, and walked toward the parking lot like she'd never intended to stay long anyway.

Rose breathed again.

By the bottom of the seventh, the Pickwick Pirate Queens were up 3-0, and the Marauders were starting to unravel. When Dani made a diving catch at third to end the inning, the stands exploded.

And Acen?

He stood and clapped.

For *them.*

For her.

After the final out, after the handshakes and cheers and the loudest rendition of "We Are the Champions" that had ever rattled the Pickwick Bend field, Rose jogged over to the bleachers to hug everyone she could get her arms around.

Declan met her halfway. She hesitated for a moment, aware of Acen behind her. Most likely watching this little encounter. She shrugged mentally. She wouldn't spend her life worrying that Acen would be jealous every time she smiled at another man. And they'd made no promises to each other. Yet.

"You came," she said, smiling at Declan.

"You told me to."

Laughing, she replied. "Didn't expect you to sit through seven innings and a heat index of ninety-eight."

"I'd sit through a double-header if it meant seeing that look on your face again."

Rose flushed.

Declan looked away as someone called his name from the parking lot. He turned back to her for a moment.

"Don't forget I want to see you again soon." He winked before turning to walk toward the parking lot where friends waited for him leaving her stomach churning.

Acen stepped into the void left by Declan and said, "Looks like charming and handsome is still interested in you."

"Don't get cute."

"Sorry." He muttered.

She hesitated, then stepped a little closer. "You handled Briana."

"She doesn't belong in this chapter."

"And what chapter is this?"

He smiled. "The one where you and I try again. Slower this time. Smarter. I'm not interested in anyone else."

Rose studied him, her heart thudding.

"Take all the time you need, Rose. I'm not going to run off again. And if you need to do some exploring first," he looked away for a moment and she could see his throat move like he was swallowing something bitter, "you do that too."

CHAPTER NINETEEN

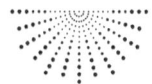

The night had settled thick and heavy over Pickwick Bend, the kind of June air that clung like a second skin. Rose sat on the porch swing with a glass of sweet tea sweating in her hand, bare feet propped on the railing. The cicadas were carrying on like they had gossip of their own. They'd been relentless this summer. And the faint glimmer of the lake showed between the pines down the hill. A lightning bug flickered past, a soft glow in the dark, and for just a second she thought about being ten years old again, barefoot in the grass catching fireflies with Riley until their mama hollered them in.

Now she was thirty-eight, and fireflies didn't answer the questions in her chest.

The screen door creaked open. Riley stepped out, a glass of tea in his hand, his ball cap pushed back like he'd given up on taming his hair. He'd come home with her after the big win to spend time with her and the team and ended up staying the night.

"Couldn't sleep?" she asked.

"Couldn't hear myself think with you pacing the kitchen half the night. When it got quiet I had to come investigate," he said, settling into the rocking chair beside her. "Figured if you're keeping the whole house awake, might as well see what's got your wheels turning."

Rose shot him a look. "Nosy much?"

"Twin perk," he said with a lazy grin, rocking back. "I can smell your trouble from a mile off. So... which flavor of headache tonight? Briana, Acen, or new boy Declan?"

Rose groaned and sank lower into the swing. "All of the above."

"That bad, huh?"

She swirled the ice in her glass, watching it melt. "Briana showed up at practice and then at the game like she owned the place. Smiled that poison smile at Acen and tried to undo the last twenty years in five minutes. Then she turned the charm on Declan. What a witch."

Riley snorted. "Yep. Heard all about it at the office. Nothing like a real estate agency for getting the best gossip. People in and out all day long." He stretched. "Sounds like Briana. Never could resist stirring a pot she had no business touching."

"She still looks... perfect," Rose admitted begrudgingly. "Not a wrinkle, not a hair out of place. And Acen

—" She broke off, shaking her head. "Acen didn't flinch. Just… stood there. Like she was a memory he'd already put in a box."

"And you?" Riley asked softly.

Rose chewed her bottom lip. "I don't know. I thought I'd be furious. Maybe a little smug if she looked worse for wear. But all I felt was… tired. Like I've been carrying the weight of her betrayal around, and I finally set it down. Only now I don't know what to do with empty hands."

Riley tipped his glass toward her. "That's something, Rosie. Means you're moving on, even if you don't know which direction yet."

She gave a hollow laugh. "Yeah, except moving on apparently means letting a new man waltz in and share my cinnamon roll in front of half the town. And, of course, Acen saw it."

Riley choked on his tea. "Declan? Lord have mercy, sis, you are really feeding the gossip mill around here lately."

"It wasn't like that," Rose protested, but her cheeks heated anyway. "He just sat down. Took a bite. But the way Acen looked at me…" She shivered, remembering. "Like I'd let him walk into a gunfight without warning him."

Riley studied her a long moment. "So which way's your heart leaning? Toward the man who broke it, or the man who hasn't had the chance yet?"

Rose stared out at the trees, the cicadas buzzing

louder. "That's the problem. One feels like home - even with all the cracks and ghosts. The other feels... easy. And I don't trust easy."

Riley rocked slowly, the creak of wood steady between them. "Maybe it isn't about easy or hard. Maybe it's about who shows up when the mess hits. Because life in Pickwick Bend isn't ever gonna be neat, sis. You just need the one who'll sit on this porch with you after the dust settles."

She blinked back sudden tears, throat tight. "When'd you get so wise?"

He smirked. "About the same time you started complicating your love life."

Rose nudged his chair with her foot, laughing through the ache. "You're impossible."

"Yep. But you'll figure it out. You always do."

For a while, they sat in silence, the night wrapping around them, both of them listening to the rhythm of the crickets and the lake. Rose didn't have her answers yet. But at least, with Riley sitting there, she didn't feel like she had to find them alone.

But the silence didn't stay comfortable for long. Rose could still feel the knot in her stomach, the tug-of-war between past and future, Acen's storm-colored eyes and Declan's easy smile. She set her tea down on the porch rail and rubbed her palms against her thighs.

"You ever wonder," she asked finally, "what our lives would've looked like if Briana had never come between me and Acen? If I'd had the chance to see what it might've been without all the lies?"

Riley rocked slow, thoughtful. "All the time. Not just for you, but for him too. He loved you, Rose. That was plain. Still might. But life's full of detours. Some folks get back on the same road. Some don't."

Rose's throat closed up. "I see him now, and part of me still aches. But another part just... doesn't trust him. Like even if he's here now, what's to stop him from running again?"

"Only way to know is to let him prove it." Riley took a sip of his tea. "Declan, though... he's not carrying that history. Doesn't mean he won't make his own mistakes, but at least you'd be starting on level ground."

Rose bit her lip. "He makes me laugh, Riley. It's been a long time since someone made me laugh just for the sake of it."

Her brother smiled softly. "Then maybe don't throw that out just yet. Lord knows, laughter's harder to come by than good catfish around here."

Rose thought about the way Declan had leaned in at the coffee shop, bold enough to swipe the icing off her cinnamon roll with his thumb. About the way Acen's jaw had tightened when he saw it.

The porch swing creaked as she shifted. "I just don't want to be the talk of the town again. Not like before. Not because of them."

Riley gave a low laugh. "Sis, you could bake a pie

wrong in this town, and it'd be the talk for a week. You think dating drama's gonna stay quiet? No chance. The question is - are you gonna let gossip decide your life?"

Rose let his words settle. The truth was, she didn't know if she was strong enough to separate her heart from Pickwick Bend's watchful eyes.

But as the night pressed in and the fireflies blinked along the yard, she knew one thing for certain: both men, Acen with his steady weight of history, and Declan with his bright new possibilities, were already tangled up in her future.

And Briana? Briana wasn't finished yet. Rose could feel it, the way you could smell rain before it fell.

CHAPTER TWENTY

Rose found herself standing in her kitchen, nervously watching the clock as the sun dipped behind the Pickwick hills, shadows stretching long and lazy across the yard. The air was heavy with the smell of baking casserole and honeysuckle drifting through the open window. She'd vacuumed the rugs, wiped down the counters twice, and even polished the little ceramic salt-and-pepper shakers shaped like ducks that had belonged to her mama.

The house was clean. The casserole was in the oven. And still, butterflies danced in her stomach like a whole team of cheerleaders.

What unsettled her most wasn't Acen himself but the fact that she was wearing lipstick. Lipstick, of all things. A muted berry shade she'd dug out of the back of her bathroom drawer, cap dusty, nearly forgotten. She hadn't bothered with lipstick in at least a year.

Not that she'd admit any of that to Acen Wheeler.

When the knock came exactly at six o'clock, not a minute earlier or later, she straightened, smoothed her skirt, and tried not to sprint for the door like a teenager with a crush.

He stood there on the porch, framed by the last gold light of the evening, holding a paper sack from the local bakery. The smell of fresh yeast rolls drifted up as soon as he shifted the bag.

"Peace offering?" she asked, arching a brow, fighting for casual when her heart had already leapt into her throat.

"Bribe," he said with that grin that had once undone every bit of sense in her. "I wasn't sure what the dress code was, but I figured carbs were always safe."

"You're not wrong," she said, stepping back and pulling the screen door wide to let him in.

Acen paused on the threshold, eyes roaming the room. His gaze softened like he'd walked straight into a memory. "It hasn't changed much since we were kids."

"I'm grateful my parents left it to me," Rose said, tucking a strand of hair behind her ear. "Lot of memories floating around these walls. And with Riley out of it, it's cleaner. He's not here to leave wet towels and stinky shoes everywhere."

That earned a chuckle. "I do kind of miss his

terrible taste in posters, though. Remember that one with the muscle car and the girl in a bikini—what was her name?"

"Trina," Rose deadpanned.

Acen snapped his fingers. "Right. I bet she's a realtor now."

"She's mayor of McNairy County."

He nearly choked on the sip of tea she'd just handed him. "You're kidding."

"Nope." Rose smirked, enjoying his shock. "Small towns: where your high school sins are just résumé bullet points."

The ease between them startled her, like no time at all had passed. She led him into the kitchen, the heart of her home, where the walls were lined with pale blue beadboard and her mama's cast-iron skillet still hung above the stove.

Acen set the bakery bag down, then, without asking, began pulling plates from the cabinet, silverware from the drawer, setting the table with a comfort that made Rose's chest ache. He moved through her kitchen as though he belonged there.

And it felt natural. Too natural. The sort of natural that could trick a lonely heart into forgetting history, forgetting scars.

And that scared her.

The casserole came out bubbling and golden, filling the room with the smell of cheese and herbs. They sat, ate the casserole, and for a while it was like nothing had ever gone wrong. They laughed about Riley's failed attempt at cutting his own hair before prom, about the year the marching band's tuba player had fainted in the Fourth of July parade from the heat. They tiptoed around the one summer they both remembered too well, the summer that had ended with Briana's triumphant smile and Rose's heart shattered.

When the plates were scraped clean and the candles she'd lit had burned low, Rose poured the two of them a glass of wine. Acen sipped his, leaning back in his chair, watching her in a way that made her skin warm.

"So," she said at last, her voice steadier than she felt. "Why now?"

He blinked. "Why what now?"

"Why come back? You could've stayed gone. Even with a blown-out knee, the pros could use a guy with your talent as a coach. You could've been anywhere. So why Pickwick Bend?"

Her words hung between them, heavy as June humidity.

Acen looked down at his hands, then back at her. He didn't answer right away.

Finally, softly: "Because I couldn't shake the feeling that I left the best parts of myself here. Because I've built a good life, Rose, a respectable one. But I never stopped wondering if the real life—the one that felt like mine—got away from me. And because..." He swallowed. "Because I hoped that maybe I still had a chance to make things right."

She stared at him, her heart thudding so loudly she swore he could hear it.

"Don't screw it up," she whispered.

"I won't," he promised.

And when he reached across the table and laid his hand over hers, she didn't pull away.

THE PICKWICK INN BAR WAS DIMLY LIT, ALL KNOTTY PINE walls and brass fixtures that had seen better days. Briana sat on a red leather stool, swirling the ice in her vodka soda, glaring at the wood-paneled wall as though it had personally betrayed her. Her reflection in the backbar mirror showed perfect makeup, perfectly styled hair, but her eyes glittered with something sharp.

Declan Rowe, seated slightly back in the corner near the big stone fireplace, had been watching her since she walked in. Not because he made a habit of watching beautiful women, though Briana was nothing if not striking, but because she radiated a kind of storm energy that drew the eye. Dangerous. Electric. Like she was plotting something.

He rose, crossing the worn carpet, and took the seat beside her. "You look like someone who just lost."

Her gaze flicked over him, cool and unimpressed. "I didn't lose. I just recalculated."

Declan chuckled. "That sounds like something someone says when they're plotting revenge."

"Maybe I am."

He lifted his glass, studying her. "Should I be concerned?"

"You?" She smirked. "No. Not unless you're planning to stand in my way."

"I try not to meddle," Declan said lightly. "But I've learned two things fast in this town: don't badmouth the Pickwick Pirate Queens, and don't mess with Rose McAllister unless you want half the county against you."

At Rose's name, Briana's smile twisted like a knife. "Funny. You sound like someone who's interested."

"Maybe I am."

She leaned in, perfume sharp and floral. "Then let me give you some free advice, Dr. Rowe. She's not as perfect as everyone pretends. And she's about to make a very familiar mistake."

Declan's easy smile dimmed, curiosity sharpening. "And you're planning to stop her?"

"I'm planning," Briana said, sliding off the stool, tossing back the last of her drink, "to make sure she doesn't forget who I am."

Her heels clicked against the wooden floor as she swayed toward the exit, leaving the faintest trace of perfume and menace behind.

Declan watched her go, unsettled. He wasn't sure whether to laugh at her dramatics or worry for Rose.

He'd come to Pickwick Bend for peace, to build a practice where he could heal dogs and cats and maybe himself after too many years in bigger cities. But clearly, he'd stumbled into a story already in motion.

And maybe, just maybe, Rose McAllister wasn't the only one who needed to watch her back.

CHAPTER TWENTY-ONE

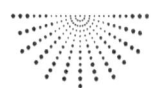

T uesday morning brought with it an ordinariness that belied the excitement of the weekend. And last night.

The June sun had just started warming the streets of Pickwick Bend, its light gilding the brick storefronts in shades of amber and honey. Main Street carried the steady hum of small-town life: the squeak of a screen door opening at The Mimosa Diner, the rhythmic clang of someone unloading crates at Fin to Fork, and the far-off laughter of kids playing in the park.

Rose stood in front of Southern Sips, waiting for the delivery guy who was, as usual, running late. The smell of coffee grounds and sugar clung to her clothes from the morning rush, and she tapped her boot against the concrete, half-listening to Cindy inside chatting with a customer about peach preserves and town politics.

Her mind, though, was somewhere else.

More specifically, on the way Acen's fingers had curled around hers the night before. Gentle. Certain. Like he wasn't trying to convince her—just remind her.

And that was maybe even more dangerous.

She blew out a breath, tilting her head back toward the sky, when a voice cut through her thoughts.

"Earth to Rose."

She blinked, snapping her gaze forward. Tasha stood there, balancing two to-go cups in a cardboard tray and looking suspiciously amused. The morning sun glinted off her earrings, and her bright floral blouse looked like something torn right from the pages of a summer catalog.

"Sorry," Rose said, straightening. "Was thinking."

"About Acen, I assume?" Tasha handed her a coffee, extra cream. Just the way Rose liked it.

"Thanks. And maybe."

Tasha smirked. "You're not as subtle as you think."

Rose gave a dry laugh. "Everyone in this town watches me like I'm a soap opera rerun."

"Because you *are* a soap opera rerun. Childhood best friend. Secret heartbreak. Blonde villainess returning from exile. All we're missing is Declan and Acen dueling it out over you at dawn and a dramatic thunderstorm confession."

"Don't tempt fate," Rose muttered, though the corner of her mouth betrayed a twitch.

They sipped in silence for a moment, the buzz of

Main Street humming around them: an old man calling his dog back from chasing a squirrel, the faint ding of the bell on The Mimosa Diner's door, the sweet smell of buttered biscuits drifting into the street.

Then Tasha said, more seriously, "Is it real this time?"

Rose stared into her coffee, watching the cream swirl like a slow storm.

"I don't know. He feels real. Like the version of himself he should've been back then. Like he's doing the work. But then I remember how fast it all fell apart. How fast *I* fell apart."

Tasha's expression softened. "Trust is a stubborn thing."

"And fragile," Rose added. "Especially when Briana's sniffing around again."

Tasha raised her brows. "Oh, she's not sniffing. She's circling. I saw her talking to Declan at the Pickwick Inn last night. They were so intent on their conversation they didn't even notice me."

Rose's head jerked up. "Declan? Why would she—?"

Tasha lifted her shoulders in an exaggerated shrug. "She knows he likes you. Everyone knows. And if she can't get to you through Acen, maybe she'll try another way."

Rose groaned, pressing her palm to her forehead. "This town needs a drama tax."

"You'd be the first one audited."

Rose gave her a sharp look, but Tasha just grinned,

clearly pleased with herself. Then, her grin faded into something a little more thoughtful.

"Truth is," Tasha said, lowering her voice, "you should probably figure out what you want from Declan before Briana stirs that pot. You've been so focused on Acen being back that you're ignoring the fact that Declan's been here this whole time. Watching, waiting, helping out when he can. He's not exactly subtle about being interested."

Rose shifted uneasily, heat creeping up her neck. "Declan's... kind. And steady. He's good for this town, opening that vet clinic. Folks like him. But I don't—" She paused, struggling to find words that didn't sound ungrateful. "I don't know if I feel that way about him. At least, not the way he seems to feel about me."

"Then you need to tread carefully," Tasha warned, her tone sharpening just a hair. "Because Declan strikes me as the type who could weather rejection just fine, but what he won't tolerate is being played. And Briana?" She whistled low. "She's going to twist anything you do into evidence that you're leading him on."

Rose scowled into her cup. "You'd think we were still sixteen the way she acts."

"Briana doesn't just want to win," Tasha said knowingly. "She wants you to lose."

The truth of that sank heavy in Rose's chest

"I am supporting you," Tasha said, holding up her cup like a toast. "By reminding you that you are at the center of the Pickwick Bend social hurricane. And Declan? He's an unknown element. Handsome, sure. Sweet with animals, obviously. But he's also new. Which means he doesn't know all the old stories. Briana can twist those any way she wants."

Rose worried her bottom lip. "So what are you saying? That I should avoid Declan altogether?"

"No." Tasha leaned closer, lowering her voice as a group of retirees shuffled by with fishing poles slung over their shoulders. "I'm saying be careful. He might mean well. He probably does. But he's still a man. And men get caught up in games they don't understand."

Rose thought about Declan's easy smile, the way he had quietly shown up at the game to cheer the team on, how he always tipped extra at Southern Sips like he wanted to make sure he was welcome. He seemed… steady. But then again, hadn't Acen seemed steady once, before that summer had wrecked everything?

She swallowed. "What if Declan's not a game player? What if he's—"

"A safe option?" Tasha finished for her.

Rose gave a weak laugh. "Yeah. Maybe."

Tasha's expression softened, though her eyes were sharp as ever. "Honey, safe isn't always the same as right. Don't use him as a shield because you're scared of getting hurt again. That's not fair to him. Or to you."

Rose let that sit heavy between them, her chest tightening. Tasha had always had a way of slicing straight to the heart of things, no matter how much Rose wanted to dance around them.

She finally sighed. "You're right. But I don't even know what I want. Acen's back, and it feels like the floor's been pulled out from under me. Declan's here, Briana's circling, and the whole town is watching like it's the county fair main event."

"Then maybe," Tasha said gently, "the only thing you can do is stop worrying about who's watching and figure out what makes you breathe easier when the dust settles. Who makes you feel like you."

Rose blinked at her, throat tight.

The delivery truck finally rumbled onto Main Street, breaking the moment. As the driver hopped down to start unloading crates of milk and sugar, Tasha patted Rose on the shoulder.

"Think on it," she said. "Acen may be the chapter you never finished, but Declan's the one standing right here in the margins. Just... don't let Briana be the one holding the pen."

And with that, she headed back into the coffee shop, leaving Rose with a knot in her chest and more questions than answers.

That evening, Rose closed the coffee shop late, exhaustion tugging at her spine as she flipped the sign and locked the door. Main Street had gone quiet, the daytime bustle traded for the hush of crickets and the occasional distant bark of a dog. Streetlamps cast soft golden halos on the pavement, and the scent of honeysuckle drifted from someone's trellis down the block.

She didn't expect to see Acen's truck parked by the curb.

Her heart gave an unsteady lurch, and before she could figure out what to do, he climbed out, holding a brown paper bag.

"You cooked?" she asked, one brow raised, suspicion mingling with surprise.

"Sort of," he said, sheepish grin tugging at his mouth. "I bribed the new diner guy into letting me take his peach cobbler. Apparently, it's won awards."

"That's not dinner."

"It's therapy," he said, holding it out like a peace offering. "I thought you might need something sweet after wrangling caffeine-hungry locals and retirees all day."

She considered, then took it. "You're lucky I didn't already eat half a chocolate cake."

"You're lucky I didn't bring a spoon and eat this in the truck alone."

Rose chuckled despite herself, and they walked to the bench outside Southern Sips. The bench was one she'd brought from the porch at home, still the forest green color her father had painted it when she was a child and kept freshly painted by her over the years. She found herself oddly grateful to share it with Acen now.

They sat down, the paper bag crackling between

them. He produced two plastic forks, and together they dug into the warm cobbler, passing it back and forth. The filling oozed with sticky sweetness, the peaches perfectly softened, the crust flaky. Rose let the sugar coat her tongue and sighed.

The sky had darkened to velvet, stars blinking faintly above as a few moths danced lazily near the lampposts.

"Your brother texted me," Acen said casually, breaking the comfortable silence.

Rose paused mid-bite. "Riley did?"

"He said, and I quote, 'Don't screw it up this time or I'll make you run sorry.'"

Rose burst out laughing, nearly choking. "That's the most brotherly blessing you're going to get."

"I'll take it."

They sat in silence a while longer, comfortable now, the kind that didn't require constant talking. Acen leaned back, stretching his long legs out, and Rose mirrored him, both of them staring at the sky as if the stars might whisper answers.

Then Rose said softly, "Do you remember that night we snuck out to watch the fireworks over the river?"

Acen smiled slowly, a hint of mischief glinting in his eyes. "You wore that red tank top."

She glanced at him, half embarrassed, half amused. "You kissed me that night."

"I wanted to kiss you again every day after that," he said without hesitation.

Her heart tripped over itself, beating faster than she wanted to admit.

She didn't say anything. Just passed him the cobbler.

But she didn't pull her hand away when his brushed hers.

And in the stillness of the summer night, it felt like a promise neither of them dared to name.

CHAPTER TWENTY-TWO

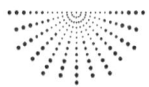

A cross town, Declan locked the door of the veterinary clinic, turning the brass key until the heavy click echoed through the empty reception area. The day's smells still lingered faintly. Antiseptic and lavender floor cleaner, the faint musk of anxious dogs. The clinic was quiet now, just the hum of the refrigerator in the back keeping vaccines cool, and the occasional settling groan of the old building.

He leaned his shoulder against the door for a moment, staring out at Main Street. The sun had set completely, leaving the sky a soft wash of indigo, the streetlamps throwing hazy circles of light on the cracked sidewalk. A couple of kids rode by on bikes, their laughter trailing behind them before fading into the quiet that always seemed to settle over Pickwick Bend after dark.

Declan slipped his stethoscope into the drawer,

then sank into the chair behind his desk, letting the leather creak under him. He should've been reviewing tomorrow's cases. Two spay surgeries, a dog with chronic allergies, a goat someone was hauling in from the edge of the county. But his mind was a thousand miles away. Or, more precisely, across town.

Rose.

He rubbed a hand over his face, exhaling slowly.

He kept circling back to the conversation with Briana the night before.

She was slick. Confident. Every word she spoke had felt like it was chosen with the precision of a scalpel. Sharp enough to cut, careful enough to leave him bleeding without realizing until too late. She hadn't needed to spell anything out. That was the trick of it. She'd dropped just enough ambiguity into the air, like smoke curling between them, making it impossible to see clearly.

And it wasn't just what she'd said. It was the way she carried herself. Like she was used to controlling the room. Like she could see the weak spots in people and press a thumb right against them.

Declan had met his fair share of confident people. Big city surgeons who strutted like gods, clients who thought money bought them knowledge. But Briana's confidence was different. It wasn't loud. It was coiled. Like she knew the right moment would come, and when it did, she'd strike.

And the worst part?

She clearly had a past with Rose.

One she wasn't denying. One she wasn't clarifying either.

Declan drummed his fingers on the desk, jaw tightening.

He didn't like being used.

But what sat heavier in his chest was the way he kept thinking about Rose anyway. The way her laughter carried just a little louder when she forgot to be careful with herself. The way her whole face lit up when she talked about her team at the coffee shop. Her second family, the thing she'd built with her own hands. The way she always seemed perched right on the edge between punching someone and forgiving them, and how damn compelling that balance was.

He wasn't the jealous type. Not normally. Jealousy felt like wasted energy, like a younger man's game. But this wasn't about jealousy, not exactly. It was about territory. And belonging. And the strange pull that had taken root in him since he first set foot in this town and looked across the street to see Rose McAllister smiling at someone else.

He knew he was the newcomer, the outsider. That was a label stamped on him whether he liked it or not. But being the outsider didn't mean he was just going to roll over and watch someone else swoop in.

Especially not someone with history and an apology smile.

Acen Wheeler.

Declan's jaw ticked again.

History was powerful. Sometimes unfairly so. And Declan couldn't compete with the fact that Acen and Rose had grown up together, had a thousand little memories layered between them like bricks in a wall. But he also knew that walls could trap as much as they protected. And from the looks of Rose lately, she wasn't sure whether to lean against Acen's wall or start knocking bricks down with her bare fists.

Declan leaned back in his chair, staring up at the ceiling.

He had time.

And patience.

But he also had a hunch that this whole thing—Acen, Briana, Rose's guarded hopefulness—was more tangled than it looked from the outside.

And tangled things?

Eventually snapped.

The rap of knuckles against the glass front door startled him out of his thoughts. Sharp, insistent. Declan glanced at the clock—just after seven. Too late for a client, and too early for trouble.

He pushed back his chair and walked out to the lobby, flicking on the small lamp near the counter before unlocking the door.

On the other side stood Luke Carter—broad-shouldered, ball cap pulled low, the kind of guy who carried himself with an ease that came from living in one place your whole life. Declan had met him a few times since moving to Pickwick Bend—at the diner, during the softball game where Rose's team had trounced the competition. Luke had a quick smile, easy humor, and the kind of handshake that made you feel like you'd known him longer than five minutes.

"Evening," Declan said, pulling the door open. "Everything okay? Don't tell me your hound found another porcupine."

Luke chuckled, stepping inside. "No, not this time. Daisy's keeping her nose clean lately. Figured I'd stop by since I saw your light on. Didn't want to interrupt if you were busy, though."

"Busy is a strong word." Declan motioned toward the chairs by the counter. "Have a seat."

Luke sat, stretching his long legs out. He glanced around the clinic, taking in the tidy reception area, the freshly painted walls, the little bulletin board with flyers about pet adoption and obedience classes. "You've done a good job fixing this place up. Old Doc Bradley let it go the last few years."

"Thanks," Declan said. He rubbed the back of his neck, hesitating before asking, "Can I be straight with you about something?"

Luke raised an eyebrow. "That sounds serious. Go on."

Declan sat across from him, leaning forward. "You've lived here a long time. You know people. You know the... dynamics."

"Meaning?" Luke asked, though the corner of his mouth tugged up like he already knew.

"Meaning Rose. Acen. Briana. And me. The newcomer who apparently walked into the middle of a story already half-written."

Luke let out a low whistle. "Yeah, that about sums it up. That what's got you burning the late evening oil here in the office? Hiding out?"

Declan sighed. "I don't like being manipulated. Briana was at the Pickwick Inn last night and we talked."

Luke raised an eyebrow but said nothing.

"She made sure I knew she and Rose had history, hinted at things but didn't spell them out. Left me with more questions than answers. Meanwhile, Acen's back in town, and everyone keeps looking at him like he's the prodigal son. And then there's Rose, who... well, she's Rose."

Luke chuckled, but his gaze was steady. "And you want to know where you fit in?"

"Exactly."

For a moment, Luke didn't answer. He leaned back in the chair, crossing his arms, looking like a man who'd seen this dance a dozen times before. "Here's the thing about Pickwick Bend," he said finally. "We've got long memories. Folks here don't forget who you were in high school, who you dated, who you broke up with. Who your folks are all the way back generations. It sticks, like gum on your shoe. Acen and Rose? That's a story most of us thought was finished years ago. Now he's back, and people are curious. Maybe hopeful."

Declan nodded slowly.

"As for Briana," Luke went on, "she's always been... ambitious. Smart, sure, but the kind of smart that wants leverage. If she's sniffing around, it's not because she cares about Rose or Acen. It's because she sees a way to tilt the board in her favor."

Declan's mouth curved grimly. "That tracks."

"And you," Luke said, pointing a finger at him, "are the outsider. Which ain't a bad thing, but it means you're playing catch-up. Folks don't quite know what to make of you yet. Some think you're good for the town. Others are waiting to see if you pack up and leave after a year."

Declan absorbed that, then asked quietly, "And Rose? What does she want?"

Luke's expression softened. "Rose wants to be happy. Trouble is, she doesn't trust it when it shows up on her porch. Not after what happened before."

Declan sat with that for a long moment.

Luke leaned forward, resting his elbows on his knees. "If you want my advice? Don't let Briana bait you, and don't waste time trying to measure yourself against Acen. You'll lose every time, because he's got the weight of history on his side. What you've got is different. You're new. Fresh. Rose might need that more than she knows."

Declan exhaled slowly, tension easing from his shoulders. "Appreciate the honesty."

"Anytime," Luke said, standing. "And for what it's worth, Doc, sometimes being the outsider gives you the clearest view of what's really going on. Don't discount that."

Declan walked him to the door, the night air cool when it swept in.

After Luke left, Declan stood in the doorway a long time, staring out at Main Street again. The lamps still burned steady, the town as quiet as before. But inside him, something had shifted.

He wasn't naïve. He knew this was a mess of old scars and new wounds. But maybe, just maybe, being the one who hadn't caused any of those scars gave him the chance to be something different.

And different might be exactly what Rose needed.

CHAPTER TWENTY-THREE

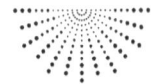

Thursday afternoon, the shop smelled like espresso and caramel, the air thick with chatter and clinking cups. A group of tourists had wandered in, still wearing Pickwick Lake T-shirts from the marina gift shop, their voices pitched just a touch too loud.

Cindy was on a tear, snapping lids onto cups with a little more force than necessary. "I swear, Rose, if the council thinks they can funnel festival money into repainting the gazebo while the parade floats look like they've been held together with duct tape and wishful thinking, then I'm—"

The bell over the door jingled, cutting her off.

Rose glanced up, expecting another cluster of customers. Instead, she saw her.

Briana.

The name hit Rose's chest like a thrown stone.

Briana stood framed in the doorway in sleek white jeans and a chambray blouse that looked like it had never seen a wrinkle. Her hair was curled to Southern perfection, glossy and swinging over her shoulders. And her expression—sugary sweet with just enough twist to curdle cream.

Rose's stomach clenched so hard she had to grab the counter for balance. The room itself seemed to pause, conversations dropping by half a note.

"Afternoon," Briana said brightly, ignoring the hush that rippled through the coffee shop.

Cindy stiffened behind the register, lips pressing into a thin line, but she said nothing.

Rose wiped her hands on a towel, buying herself a breath before she straightened slowly. Her throat was dry, but her voice came out steady. "Can I help you?"

"Oh, I don't know." Briana's smile sharpened. "I thought maybe I'd grab a coffee. Support a local business. Small-town girl and all."

Rose stepped out from behind the counter, sliding into the space between Briana and Cindy like a buffer. "We're pretty busy."

"I'll be quick." Briana's eyes sparkled like she knew exactly what she was doing.

She waited patiently at the register while Cindy rang her up, black coffee, no cream, no sugar. The drink of someone with a blackmail folder in her purse and no time for nonsense.

Rose knew it was all theater. Briana could've gone to the café down the block, or the new smoothie bar by the boutique hotel. Could've picked anywhere but *here*. She hadn't come for coffee. She'd come for an audience.

When the cup slid across the counter, Briana lifted it with both hands, perfectly manicured nails catching the light.

"You know, Rose," she said casually, "it's funny how things always come back around, isn't it?"

Rose's jaw ached as she clenched it. "*Some* things should've stayed gone."

Briana smiled, sweet as poison. "That's one way to look at it. Or maybe this town has a way of remembering what's real. What's meant to be."

The words slid under Rose's skin, hot and sharp. She opened her mouth, but Cindy beat her to it—dropping a spoon onto the counter with a clatter that echoed through the shop.

A couple of heads swiveled, whispering.

Rose ignored them, her pulse pounding. "If you're referring to Acen—"

"Oh, honey," Briana interrupted with a soft laugh. "*I'm* not the one trying to rewrite history."

The words dripped with insinuation. Acen's name was a knife Briana twisted with a practiced hand.

Cindy's nostrils flared, but she kept her voice even. "We've got orders piling up, Rose."

Translation: don't let her bait you.

But it was hard, standing there with every nerve sparking like a live wire.

Briana, of course, wasn't finished. She took a slow sip of her coffee—like she was tasting victory more than caffeine—then leaned just slightly closer. "Anyway. I'm on my way to meet Declan. He's helping me find someone reputable to buy a registered poodle puppy from. You know how hard it is to find someone around here for things like that."

Rose's pulse spiked. Declan? Working with *her*?

Her grip tightened on the towel until the fabric bit into her palm. "You're working with Declan?"

"Mm-hmm." Briana hummed the sound, soft and satisfied. "He's been so helpful. That man notices everything."

The double-meaning wasn't subtle.

The coffee shop was too small, too hot. Rose's breath caught in her chest as if Briana had reached across the counter and pressed a finger directly over her heart.

"Well," Briana said after a pause that stretched too long, "I should go. Lots to do. This town isn't going to impress itself."

She turned, hips swaying as she walked out, strappy sandals clicking against the tile. The door swung shut behind her with a sound that felt like a gunshot in the silence that followed.

Cindy blew out a sharp breath. "That woman has the emotional range of a viper in a sundress."

Rose stared at the closed door, throat tight. "She's just warming up."

The buzz of the shop slowly resumed, customers whispering to one another, pretending not to watch Rose. But she felt every glance, every unspoken *bless your heart* aimed her way. This was Pickwick Bend, after all—where gossip traveled faster than cell service.

Cindy nudged her gently with her elbow. "Ignore her. She's only here for one thing."

Rose shook her head, still staring at the door. "No. She's here for three things. Acen. Declan. And trouble."

"Then she's gonna get herself a full plate," Cindy muttered.

But the words didn't settle Rose's stomach. Not when she thought about Declan, steady, kind Declan, caught in Briana's orbit.

The towel slipped from her hand onto the counter. For the first time all day, Rose forgot the line of customers, forgot Cindy's rant about the festival, forgot everything except the storm Briana had just carried in like a trophy.

Because storms didn't come to Pickwick Bend without tearing up roots.

And Rose had the distinct feeling that this one wasn't passing quick.

CHAPTER TWENTY-FOUR

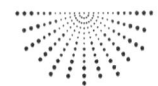

That evening, after a full day at the coffee shop, Rose found herself pacing in her living room. The hardwood floors creaked faintly beneath her bare feet, each step marking out the rhythm of her restless thoughts. The windows were open, the evening breeze drifting through lace curtains, carrying with it the faint scent of honeysuckle and damp earth. It should've been calming. Instead, the quiet only made her thoughts louder.

The same questions spun in her mind, a carousel she couldn't step off.

Why was Briana targeting Declan?

What was her endgame?

What exactly was she implying with her comments about rewriting history?

Rose wrapped her arms around herself, standing

near the mantle where old family photos were lined up in mismatched frames. One caught her eye—her and Riley at twelve, grinning with matching missing front teeth. Another, her mother in a Sunday dress, holding a younger Rose in her lap. Those memories were supposed to be safe, untouched by Briana's sharp tongue or carefully crafted drama. But lately, even the most ordinary things felt like they had shadows lurking behind them.

She turned away, moving to the couch and sinking down. Her body was tired from the long shift. Coffee spills, Cindy's rants about the town council's poor budgeting for the fall festival, and the subtle hum of gossip that ran like electricity through every small-town establishment. But her mind wouldn't quiet.

Acen had said he was done with Briana. Had shown it, too—his words steady, his choices clear. But Briana wasn't the type to accept "no." She was the type to pry open old wounds, wedge herself in like a splinter, and smile while doing it. And now she was circling Declan like a hawk over new prey.

Rose rubbed her temples, the pads of her fingers pressing into the tension that had settled there.

Should she warn Declan? He was a grown man, after all. He'd already proved he wasn't naive. Thoughtful, yes, but not blind. Still... the thought of him getting dragged into Briana's game made her stomach twist. Declan didn't deserve that. He deserved a clean slate, a chance to plant roots in

Pickwick Bend without somebody weaponizing the past against him.

And selfishly - Rose admitted it - she didn't want Briana using Declan to needle her. She didn't want Briana tainting something that felt, for once, like possibility instead of regret.

Her phone buzzed on the coffee table, making her jump.

She leaned forward and picked it up. A text from Acen.

You free? I've got news. Meet me at the dock?

Rose stared at the words, heart thudding. She hesitated, chewing on her bottom lip. This was dangerous territory. Meeting Acen at the dock pulled on a thread of the past she wasn't sure she wanted to unravel. But her curiosity, her fear of what Briana might've done now, outweighed her caution.

She slipped on her sandals, grabbed her keys, and locked the door behind her.

THE DRIVE ACROSS TOWN WAS SHORT, BUT IT GAVE HER too much time to think. The streets of Pickwick Bend were quiet this late in the evening, porch lights glowing, dogs barking distantly as if to announce her passing. She rolled down her window, the thick summer night pressing in.

The dock behind the high school hadn't changed in years. Locals fished there during the day, kids snuck beers at night, and once upon a time it had been her spot with Acen. That thought alone made her chest tighten.

When she pulled into the gravel lot, she spotted him immediately. Acen leaned against one of the wooden posts, arms crossed, his frame backlit by the silvery wash of moonlight on the water. His stance was casual, but she knew him well enough to see the tension in his shoulders.

He turned as she approached, pushing off the post. "Sorry for the short notice," he said, voice low.

"What's going on?" she asked, her sandals scuffing against the boards of the dock.

Without answering, he pulled a folded piece of paper from his back pocket and handed it to her. His fingers brushed hers briefly - warm, solid.

She unfolded it, the paper crinkling in the quiet night. Her eyes scanned the typed words, and she froze.

Ask Rose McAllister what really happened the summer Acen left. Some of us haven't forgotten who she used to be.

Her blood ran cold. The night sounds, the chirp of crickets, the gentle lap of water against the dock, faded into a hollow silence.

"Where did you get this?" she whispered.

"Someone dropped it off at the garage," Acen said, his jaw tight. "Addressed to me."

Her grip on the letter tightened, the edges cutting into her fingers. "You think it's from Briana?"

"I don't think," he said softly. "I *know*. It's just her style to pull something like this."

Rose exhaled shakily, her throat tight. Of course it was Briana. This had her fingerprints all over it. She was twisting the past, digging up pain that should've been buried long ago.

Her hands trembled slightly, and she hated that Acen could see it.

"She's not just trying to ruin this," he said, watching her closely. "She's trying to rewrite the past. And if we don't face it head-on, she's going to win."

Rose looked out over the water. The river stretched wide and endless, reflecting the moon in broken shards, like glass cracked but still holding together. The sight was beautiful and fragile all at once, and it mirrored exactly how she felt.

Her voice came out low. "She's right about one thing."

Acen tilted his head. "What's that?"

"There's more to that summer than I've ever told anyone." The words slipped out before she could catch them, heavy with meaning, with memory.

Acen's gaze didn't waver. "Then tell me," he said, steady, unwavering. "All of it."

Silence hung heavy between them, filled only by the creak of the dock and the distant croak of a frog along the bank.

Acen touched her arm. "If Briana wants to drag the

past into the light, let her. But she doesn't get to define it. You do. Whatever it is she thinks she knows."

Rose blinked against the sting in her eyes. She wanted to believe him. Wanted to believe the past didn't have to be a weapon in Briana's hands.

But part of her was terrified. Terrified that once everything came out, even Acen wouldn't look at her the same way again.

CHAPTER TWENTY-FIVE

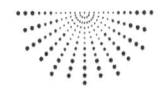

The dock creaked beneath them as a breeze stirred off the river, cool and carrying the scent of rain. The river spread out in both directions, a long silver ribbon in the twilight. A frog croaked somewhere near the bank, and crickets sang their rising chorus. In the distance, faint thunder rumbled—a storm building but not yet here.

Rose didn't sit. She couldn't. The wooden bench on the dock looked too permanent, too much like a place to settle. Instead, she stood at the edge, arms crossed tight across her chest like she could hold in the memories if she just braced hard enough. Her body carried the tension of someone holding the levee against years' worth of floodwater.

Acen stayed quiet.

He knew this wasn't easy. His arms rested loosely at his sides, but his gaze was steady, patient. He wasn't going to force her. He'd learned something about silence in the years he'd been gone. It had weight. Sometimes it was heavier than words.

Finally, Rose exhaled. A long, shaky breath that left her shoulders trembling.

"That summer..." she began, her voice distant, thinned by memory, "I was supposed to go to college with Riley. We had this whole plan. We'd leave Pickwick Bend together, head to Knoxville, share an apartment, build new lives. He'd coach, I'd bake or teach or do something other than be the girl who never left town."

Acen nodded slowly. He remembered how close the twins had always been, almost like one mind split into two bodies. Their future had seemed like a joint package, neatly wrapped and ready to go. He remembered teasing Rose once, back when they were eighteen, about how she and Riley ought to print business cards with their names side by side.

"But you didn't go." A premonitory chill chased down his spine. He'd never really thought about that before. Why Rose hadn't left for Knoxville with Riley the way they'd discussed all senior year.

"I didn't go," she said, her eyes locked on the water, the moon's reflection quivering on the surface. "And everyone assumed it was because of what happened with you. That you broke my heart, and I couldn't handle leaving. That I stayed behind to lick my wounds and pretend I was better off. Even Riley believed that."

The way she said it—flat, with a bitter edge—made Acen's chest tighten.

"That's not what happened?" he asked gently.

Her jaw clenched so hard the muscles trembled. "No. You leaving broke something, sure. But I could've handled that. I could've gone on. What I couldn't handle… was what came after."

Her gaze flicked to him, sharp and pained, before drifting back to the water.

"Briana wasn't just my best friend back then, Acen. She was like a sister. Remember? We were inseparable from second grade until that summer. I told her everything. Including that I was in love with you."

The words landed heavy between them.

He blinked, caught off guard, breath faltering. "I—I didn't know—"

"She did," Rose said bitterly, her voice cracking under the strain. "And a week later, she kissed you at graduation. And you let her."

Acen's face fell, guilt washing over him in waves. "I didn't know she knew. I thought—I thought you didn't feel that way after what she told me that night. That you were done with me and didn't know how to break it to me. That you and Riley were heading to Knoxville and everything we'd planned together was just kid stuff. I was stupid. I thought—"

"You thought I didn't care." Rose's arms tightened across her chest, nails digging into her arms. "I was eighteen. I didn't know how to say it. But I trusted her. And she used it to wedge herself between us."

The weight of betrayal carried years of rust, but it was still sharp as a blade.

Acen rubbed the back of his neck, his voice low. "She told me you were done with me. That you'd moved on. That Riley had said he didn't want us together but didn't want to tell me."

Rose gave a strangled laugh, one that wasn't laughter at all. "I never moved on. I tried to hate you, and I hated her more. But it wasn't even the worst part."

She stepped back, her body taut like a bowstring, arms still crossed as though shielding her heart.

"Right after you left," she said softly, "I found out I was pregnant."

The words hung in the air like thunder without lightning, a pressure that made the night seem stiller, darker.

Acen froze.

"What?" His voice cracked.

Rose looked away, staring at the water as though it might swallow her confession. "I didn't tell anyone. Not even Riley. I was eighteen. I hadn't told you how I felt. I was terrified. And then... I lost the baby."

Acen's face drained of color. He opened his mouth, then closed it, searching for words that didn't exist. His chest rose and fell in short, sharp breaths.

"I didn't know," he whispered finally, voice breaking on the syllables.

"You weren't here," she said, not cruel, just hollow. "And Briana was. For a few weeks, at least, until she left for college too. And she knew. She figured it out and made it clear that if I ever tried to tell anyone what she'd done to break us up, she'd spread lies about me all over town. That I was reckless. That I was trying to trap you. I was grieving and alone and so full of shame that I just… shut down. I canceled my college plans. I stayed here. And I stopped letting anyone in."

The silence that followed was suffocating. Even the crickets seemed to hush, the whole riverbank leaning in to listen.

Acen's throat worked as he swallowed, his fists curling at his sides. Anger, hot and helpless, burned in his veins. Anger at himself for not being there. Anger at Briana for twisting everything pure into something rotten.

Finally, he stepped forward. Gently. Like approaching a skittish deer.

"I should've come back sooner," he said, his voice thick. "I should've asked questions. I should've fought for us." He reached out and touched her cheek. "Did you ever tell Riley?"

She nodded. "A few years ago. He was pretty pissed I'd kept it from him all that time."

"I'm so sorry. I know I've said that multiple times already."

"You didn't know."

"But I do now." His voice cracked. "Rose, I'm so sorry. For all of it. For being blind, for leaving, for not giving you a reason to believe in me."

She looked at him then, really looked—at the boy she'd loved and the man he'd become. His eyes were rimmed with unshed tears, his jaw tight with regret. And her own eyes stung, the tears she'd been holding back threatening to spill.

"I didn't want your pity," she whispered.

He reached for her hand, slow and careful.

"I'm not giving you pity," he said. His voice was firm now, steady. "I'm giving you the truth. I love you. I never stopped loving you."

The words soaked into her like rain after a drought, seeping deep into soil that had long since cracked. For a heartbeat, she let herself imagine it—that love was enough, that it could patch over the past like a quilt over worn boards.

But love wasn't enough—not by itself.

"Then help me," she said, her voice low but fierce. "Help me take my life back. Help me take her down."

Acen squeezed her hand, his grip warm and solid, grounding her against the storm that still raged inside.

"Whatever you need," he said.

The dock groaned beneath their weight, the river whispering against the pilings. Overhead, the first scatter of raindrops fell, soft against the water, darkening the planks.

CHAPTER TWENTY-SIX

Rose woke with a clarity she hadn't felt in years. For so long, her pain had been something private. She'd lived with it hidden under layers of baked goods, hometown obligations, stubborn pride, and the rhythm of ordinary days. It was safer that way. Pickwick Bend was a town where nothing stayed quiet for long.

But now, her secret wasn't buried anymore—not completely. Acen knew. Something he'd had every right to know all those years ago, but she'd been too young and scared to tell him.

The fear of what Briana might do. What she had already started doing. That burned hotter than the shame itself. Rose had kept her silence for so long, but she wasn't naïve. Briana wasn't bluffing. She was a woman who thrived on attention, on twisting stories into something sharp enough to cut. And if Briana decided to make Rose's secret public? The whole town would know before sundown, whispered between church pews and repeated at the Piggly Wiggly checkout line.

Rose was done hiding. But being done hiding and being ready to face Briana's brand of cruelty weren't the same thing. The whole town didn't need to know that part of her story.

She dressed quickly, needing movement, needing distraction. The coffee shop gave her both. By the time the sun lifted over the horizon, she was unlocking the back door, setting out muffins, and forcing herself into the comfort of routine. The bell above the front door chimed often—farmers in for their morning caffeine, teachers with lesson plans tucked under their arms, retirees who lingered just to talk.

It was almost enough to keep her mind busy. Almost.

The bell rang again, and this time it wasn't a customer.

Riley stepped inside, not even bothering with hello. His expression was a mixture of weariness and protectiveness, like a man bracing for a blow.

"You told him," he said flatly.

Rose froze, her hand halfway to the stack of cups. "I did."

He crossed his arms, every inch of him the older brother—even if they were twins. "I figured, when he texted me at midnight asking if I ever knew... anything."

Her heart stumbled. "And what did you say?"

"I said it wasn't my story to tell." Riley's gaze softened, his posture easing. "But I also told him I'd sure as hell stand beside it. Beside you."

The relief hit her like a wave, leaving her shoulders sagging. "Thank you."

"You okay?" he asked.

"No," she admitted. "But I'm getting there."

Riley studied her, chewing on the inside of his cheek like he always did when he wanted to push harder but knew better. Finally, he nodded. "Good. You always get there eventually. Stubborn as hell, just like Dad."

That made her smile faintly, despite everything. "Mom used to say we came out fighting."

"You did," Riley said, snagging a muffin from the counter. "And now you've got Acen in your corner again."

Rose's hand faltered over the chip bags. "I don't know what that means yet."

Riley raised an eyebrow, giving her a look that said he'd been seeing through her since they were kids. "Come on. You're not fooling anyone. Least of all me."

She swallowed. "I'm not trying to fool anyone. But you know me. I can't just sit still and wait for Briana's next move. I need to do something. I need to take control before she twists this into something uglier than it already is."

Riley tore off a piece of muffin, his jaw hard. "Then start with the truth. Your truth. Don't let her weaponize it."

His words hung in the air long after he left.

As she straightened the pen holder next to the cash register, she noticed an envelope tucked under it. Curious, she pulled it out. No writing on the front, so she slit the seal to figure out what it could be.

Her blood froze when she read the words in bold black print on a half sheet of white paper.

People put you on a pedestal, Rose, but if the truth about your past came out, they'd think twice. A girl who hides something that big doesn't deserve their trust.

Carefully, face strategically blank, she pushed the paper back into the envelope. A quick glance around the coffee shop showed no one looking her way.

When had Briana hidden the letter? Rose had no doubt about the author.

Time to call in reinforcements.

War was coming.

LATER THAT DAY, ROSE SAT ON TASHA'S BACK PORCH with Acen. Riley and Tasha, the three of them gathered around an old wooden table scarred from years of backyard barbecues and impromptu card games. The summer afternoon smelled faintly of honeysuckle and charcoal from a neighbor's grill.

Rose dropped the anonymous letter onto the table like it was poison. "Tash, I'm in trouble, and I need your help."

Tasha read the note, frowning at the typewritten words. "Briana?"

Rose nodded. "Right the first time."

Tasha frowned. "This is bold. Is she planning on sending this kind of thing around town? That's not just stirring the pot—that's trying to burn the whole kitchen down."

"And she's playing Declan," Rose added, her throat tight. "I don't know how far she's gone with him, but she's doing it to get under my skin. He doesn't even know he's a pawn."

"Declan's sharp," Acen said. "He'll figure it out. He's already wary of her."

Rose shook her head. "Not if she twists the story before I get a chance to stop her. You both know how quick folks around here are to believe the worst. If she paints me as weak, reckless, manipulative..." Her voice cracked. "That's the version of me people will remember."

Anger burned in Riley's eyes. "Why are you even trying to be reasonable about this. She's out for blood and it's yours she's after. You have to take her down regardless of anything else. She's trying to ruin you."

Her twin was ready to take Briana down and damn the consequences to anyone else

Acen opened his mouth, but Rose stopped whatever he'd been about to say by placing her hand on Riley's arm. "Don't, Riley. Don't be like her. Don't ruin everything for the sake of being the one that wins at any cost. I'm not that kind of person. Never have been and don't intend to let Briana be the one that makes me become that kind of person. But I also don't intend to let her ruin everything I've built for myself here."

Tasha leaned back in her chair, arms crossed. "So what's the plan? You going to out her? Call her out at church or the softball field and make a scene?"

"No," Rose said firmly. "That's exactly what she wants—more drama. Another story to spin."

"Then what?" Tasha pressed.

Rose exhaled, her hands tightening around her coffee mug. "I don't know yet. We need to find some way to prove she's been lying, scheming, manipulating. She's smart, but she's also cocky. Eventually, she'll trip. And when she does, we'll be ready."

Acen leaned forward, steady and solid beside her. "She's counting on your silence, Rosie. But she doesn't get to use your past like a hammer. Not if we stand together."

For a moment, Rose just looked at him. Years of grief and anger swirled inside her, but beneath it all, there was something steadier. Resolve. She wasn't carrying this weight alone.

And that was the difference.

CHAPTER TWENTY-SEVEN

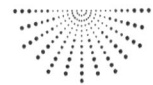

The next few days blurred into a rhythm of planning and watching. Rose couldn't walk down Main Street without wondering who Briana had already whispered to. She couldn't pour coffee without wondering if someone's curious glance was rooted in gossip. Every polite smile felt like it carried a question she didn't want to answer.

But she wasn't running, but the waiting game definitely had big drawbacks. She thought an actual sword hanging over her head might be preferable to this invisible assault.

Practice for the next game in the tournament was her savior. Thursday night she stood in the dugout, nerves strung tight as she gave the girls the plays to start off.

The air hummed with late summer heat, the kind that clung to your skin even as the sun sank lower over the horizon. A sweet breeze blew occasionally across the field stirring up red dust, mixing with the steady thud of balls hitting leather gloves. Rose breathed it in like medicine. The diamond was familiar ground, a place where problems could shrink to nothing more than bases, bats, and hustle.

"Alright, ladies," Rose called, clapping her hands together. "Let's run double plays until they're second nature. No hesitation."

The team scattered into their positions, voices lifting in chatter and encouragement. Rose's chest tightened, not from the drill but from the folded note that still sat on her kitchen counter at home. The words burned through her like acid. She'd thrown herself into work at the coffee shop, then straight into practice, anything to keep her mind from replaying the message.

Acen stood near third base, hat pulled low, his whistle hanging loosely around his neck. He barked out instructions with an ease that came from years of playing, his eyes flicking toward Rose now and then like he could read her silence. When one of the girls overthrew to first, he jogged over, corrected her stance, and offered a quick grin. The team had warmed to him faster than Rose had expected, and watching him move among them—patient, steady, encouraging—pinched something tender inside her.

"Keep your glove down, Maggie! That ball's not going to wait for you to get ready!" Rose shouted, her voice sharper than usual. A couple of the girls exchanged wary glances.

Tasha leaned against the dugout railing, sipping from a water bottle, her dark eyes never leaving Rose. She caught the edge in Rose's tone, the way her jaw stayed tight even when the girls pulled off a flawless double play.

"You alright?" Tasha murmured when Rose passed by to grab her clipboard.

"Fine," Rose said too quickly, scribbling notes she didn't need.

"Mm-hmm." Tasha's look said she wasn't buying it.

Rose turned away, focusing on the crack of the bat as one of the girls sent a clean line drive into left field. The cheer that went up around the field loosened something inside her, but only for a moment. No matter how hard she tried to drown in the rhythm of the game, Briana's shadow lingered at the edges.

Acen caught her eye from across the diamond. He tipped his cap, subtle but sure, like a reminder: *I'm here. You're not alone in this fight.*

Rose lifted her chin, squared her shoulders, and blew her whistle. "Alright, let's run it again! Tournament's not going to wait on us!"

The girls groaned, but they hustled back into position, dust rising around their cleats. Rose clung to the noise, the movement, the smell of the field. For now, at least, she could pretend the only battle that mattered was the one between the bases.

When she lay awake at night, though, doubt crept in. What if Briana beat her to it? What if the version of her secret that hit the streets was the one Briana had been sharpening for years? In a town like Pickwick Bend, reputation wasn't just something you wore—it was stitched into your name.

The fear was real. But so was her determination.

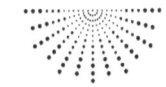

CHAPTER TWENTY-EIGHT

Declan stood behind the counter of his veterinary office, sorting through a box of dog vitamins when the door opened and Briana swept in.

She wore a cream-colored dress and a smile that could melt asphalt.

"I brought you something," she said, holding up a folder.

"What is it?"

"Just... some context," she said innocently. "A few things I thought you should see. About Rose."

Declan didn't take it.

"What kind of things?"

"Oh, nothing dramatic." She placed the folder on the counter. "Just history. A few diary passages, some old messages. Little reminders that the version of Rose you're seeing now? It's not the full picture."

He narrowed his eyes. "Why would you give me this?"

"Because I like you," she said simply. "And I hate watching good men get dragged into messy lies. I've been on the losing end of that story before."

"Were you?" he asked, coldly.

She tilted her head. "Are you saying you *don't* want to know the truth?"

Declan looked down at the folder. His jaw flexed.

"No," he said finally. "I want to hear it from *her*. Not you."

Briana's smile faltered just a hair. Then it came back, brighter than ever.

"Suit yourself. Just don't say I didn't try."

She turned and walked out, heels clicking like punctuation marks.

Declan stared at the folder.

And even though he didn't open it—

Doubt had already crept in.

ROSE WAS RESTOCKING THE COFFEE SHOP'S MUFFIN BIN when the bell above the door rang. She looked up with a practiced smile—one that faltered the moment she saw Declan standing there.

He looked tired. More serious than usual. And he was holding a manila folder.

Her stomach dropped.

"Hey," she said cautiously. "Everything okay?"

Declan didn't answer right away. He stepped inside and let the door swing shut behind him. The bakery was quiet—between lunch and after dinner rush, with only the hum of the cooler to fill the silence.

"I think you already know why I'm here," he said.

She wiped her hands on a towel. "That folder. Briana?"

He nodded once.

"She came by the office. Told me you weren't being honest. Said this"—he lifted the folder—"would show me who you really are."

Rose swallowed hard. "Did you read it?"

"No," he said. "Not yet."

Her breath caught.

"But I thought about it," he admitted. "Because I like you, Rose. A lot. And I didn't want to believe she had anything I didn't already know."

She leaned against the counter, feeling every ounce of the weight she carried.

"She's trying to ruin me," Rose said quietly. "She's always been good at it. She was my best friend, and when she realized I loved Acen back in high school, really loved him, she made sure to get to him and mess that up with a pack of lies. And when he left... when everything fell apart, she didn't stop. She twisted the story. Kept twisting it, hoping it would break me."

Declan nodded slowly. "Acen said something

happened. That she was behind it. But it's hard to know what's truth and what's just... emotion."

"You want the truth?" Rose's voice was steadier now. "I was pregnant. I lost the baby. And she knew— she *used* it against me to keep me quiet."

Declan's expression shifted from skeptical to stunned. "You... what?"

"I never told anyone," she said. "I couldn't. I was ashamed. I thought I'd done something wrong. And when Briana made it clear she'd turn it into a town scandal, I just... shut it all down. I stayed here. I let her win."

Declan's gaze dropped to the folder in his hands.

"I didn't want to believe her," he said. "But I also didn't want to feel like a fool."

"You're not," Rose said softly. "But you deserve the full story. Even if it's ugly."

He looked at her for a long moment. Then, without a word, he turned and walked to the trash can near the door.

He dropped the folder in without opening it.

And walked back to her.

"I believe you," he said.

Rose blinked. "Even without proof?"

"Especially without it. Because it's not just what you said—it's how you said it. And because I've seen who Briana is when she thinks no one's watching."

Her throat tightened.

"I'm sorry she tried to use me," he added. "And I'm sorry I didn't come to you first."

"You're here now."

He gave her a small, sincere smile. "And I'm not going anywhere."

CHAPTER TWENTY-NINE

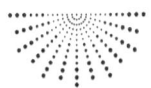

T he Pickwick Yacht Club on a Thursday night was the closest thing the town had to sophistication. Its heavy velvet curtains blocked out the streetlamps, the chandeliers gleamed soft gold, and the white-tablecloth tables glowed like snowdrifts in the low lighting. People came for the steak, but they stayed for the talk. Everyone knew that.

Briana leaned over a glass of wine, her voice low and sugar-slicked as she chatted with Marlene Greaves —who just so happened to run the town's gossip column.

"Rose?" Briana said with a tinkling laugh. "Oh, bless her heart. She's been through so much. But you know what they say—some people thrive on drama. I just hope she knows how to protect her business. Small-town reputations are so delicate."

Marlene leaned in. "What are you saying, dear?"

Briana offered a helpless shrug. "I'd never say a word out of turn. But... some people might want to know who they're buying their coffee from. Especially if there are secrets. Old... scandals."

She sipped her wine, eyes glinting.

If she couldn't tear Rose down with the truth, she'd do it with suggestion.

The kind that stuck harder than fact.

And Briana knew how to work a room.

She'd chosen her spot carefully, near enough to the bar that anyone waiting on a drink could overhear just a note of her conversation with Marlene, but far enough back that it looked private, intimate. It was theater, every drop of it, and she played her role like a woman born for the stage.

Marlene, bless her nosy little heart, was leaning forward, her pearl necklace gleaming under the light. She smelled blood, and Briana was more than happy to give her the faintest taste.

"You don't mean..." Marlene whispered, her eyes wide.

"I don't mean anything," Briana said smoothly, her tone laced with the same false innocence she'd been perfecting since high school. "I only think about the community. How we all depend on each other. Coffee, fellowship, Sunday mornings after church—it's all connected, isn't it?"

Marlene's lips pursed thoughtfully. "It is."

"And Rose, well... she's done a wonderful job

building that shop. I admire her grit. But sometimes grit hides other things. Painful things. Things people might rather forget."

Marlene reached for her glass, nearly sloshing the wine down her sleeve. "You've got me on pins and needles, Briana."

Briana gave a demure laugh, the kind meant to look like she was brushing it all aside when she was really feeding the flame. "Oh, I shouldn't say another word. Wouldn't want to add to the rumor mill. You know how this town can be."

Marlene nodded slowly, though her expression told a different story. The gossip column she typed up every week was the most widely read part of the county paper. A hint from Briana tonight would ripple out by Sunday morning, carried from pew to pew, whispered over casseroles at fellowship lunch.

Exactly as Briana intended.

By the time Briana left the club, her heels clicking confidently against the brick walkway, the match had been struck.

AND THE NEXT MORNING, THE FIRST WHISPER HIT.

It wasn't loud, not at first.

A woman at the farmers market leaned toward her friend as Rose passed by, murmuring behind her hand. Their eyes darted away too quickly when Rose offered a polite smile.

At the coffee shop, Rose caught a group of teenagers pausing outside her window before ducking in. Their laughter seemed sharper, though no words were clear enough to grab hold of.

Even at the church parking lot, where Rose had parked to drop off muffins for a fundraiser, the hush fell thick when she walked past two women arranging flowers for the sanctuary. One of them offered a too-bright "Good morning!" but her eyes flickered with something sharper.

It was subtle.

But it was spreading.

CHAPTER THIRTY

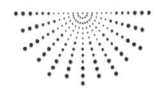

R ose felt it in her bones.

She'd always been able to read a room. A survival instinct, honed through years of keeping her head high while life tried to chip away at her. She could sense when laughter was genuine, when kindness was real, and when a conversation shifted the second she walked out of earshot.

By noon, the whispers were everywhere. Not enough to confront, not enough to pin down, but enough to knot her stomach tight.

She carried mugs to the dishwasher and heard it in the hush of conversation at the corner table. She stepped onto Main Street for a delivery and caught the subtle arch of brows, the way voices softened when she passed by. It was like walking through fog—she couldn't see the shape of it, couldn't catch a word outright, but she knew it was there, thick and clinging.

Back at the coffee shop, she wiped down the counter twice, her rag catching on the same scratch in the wood.

The scratch had been there since the first week she opened. A delivery man had dragged in a heavy box, set it down too hard, and left the gouge. She'd meant to fix it, but after a while it became familiar, like the wrinkles in her favorite quilt—imperfections that belonged to her. Today, though, it snagged at her every time she dragged the rag across, pulling her back to the same spot again and again.

Tasha noticed, leaning over from the pastry case where she'd been helping arrange lemon bars and pecan tarts for the afternoon rush.

"You're gonna rub the finish clean off if you keep that up," Tasha said softly.

Rose forced a laugh. "Guess I'm restless."

"Guess you're lying."

The words landed gentle, but firm. Tasha had a way of cutting straight to the truth without raising her voice.

Rose continued to apply the rag to the already clean counter like her life depended on it. The wood creaked faintly beneath her pressure, her knuckles whitening around the damp cloth.

"Why?" Tasha asked after a moment. "Rose. Why is she doing this?"

Rose stopped. The rag stilled in her hand. Slowly,

she looked up, anguish flickering across her eyes before she could mask it.

"Because she can," she whispered, her voice sharper than she intended. She swallowed hard, tried again. "Because she wants Acen back and he made it clear to her that he's not interested. So, the only thing she can think to do is ruin my life because he wants me instead."

The words hung between them like smoke. Heavy, cloying, impossible to wave away.

She met Tasha's steady gaze, and for a moment the weight of it almost undid her. Tasha's brown eyes were unwavering, calm as a steady current under storm-tossed water. They reminded Rose of long summer evenings sitting side by side on the bleachers, or late-night phone calls when heartbreak felt unbearable. Those eyes had seen her through everything. And now, they saw right through her again.

But Rose pressed her lips together, shook her head, and turned back to the counter.

Because admitting what she suspected. That Briana had started something. That her oldest secret was suddenly dangling over her head again. It felt like handing Briana the win.

And Rose McAlister didn't hand out wins.

The bell over the shop door jingled, scattering the thick silence. A pair of women from church stepped in, their perfume cloying, their polite smiles too sharp.

"Afternoon," Rose called brightly, her voice smooth

as honey, though her stomach twisted. She tucked the rag away and straightened the napkin stack.

The women ordered two cappuccinos and a slice of hummingbird cake, and as Rose prepared them, she felt the weight of their eyes. Not cruel, not even openly suspicious. Just curious. Curious in that small-town way that meant their interest wasn't friendly.

She set the drinks down with her best practiced smile. "Y'all enjoy now."

They murmured thanks, retreated to a corner booth, and bent close over their cups. Rose didn't have to hear the words to know her name was in their mouths.

Tasha came to stand at her side, arms crossed, her shoulder brushing Rose's. "They're not worth it."

"Maybe not," Rose muttered. "But they'll be here every Sunday after church and sometimes during the week, and I'll feel it."

"Then hold your head higher." Tasha squeezed her arm. "They can't shame what you don't let 'em touch."

Rose wanted to believe that. Lord, she wanted to. But inside, her secret burned like a coal. One careless breath from Briana, and it could ignite into a blaze she'd never outrun.

That night, after locking the shop, Rose lingered alone at one of the tables, staring at the chalkboard menu. The day's specials were still scrawled in pastel pink and blue, the neat handwriting looping across the board. She tried to read the words, but all she saw was the reflection of her own fear.

She poured herself a cup of coffee—lukewarm, bitter—and sat with it until the shadows in the corners of the shop stretched long and heavy.

Pickwick Bend was supposed to be her safe place. After years of struggling, of mistakes and rebuilding, this coffee shop was her proof she could stand on her own. She'd carved out something steady, something good. And Briana was trying to rip it from her, not by truth but by suggestion.

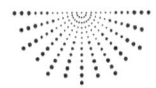

CHAPTER THIRTY-ONE

At her home out in the county, the home where she'd grown up and become bitter about her prospects until she decided to change her own future, Briana perched at her vanity, painting her lips a glossy red as she hummed along to the radio.

The little house creaked with familiarity, every corner a reminder of the years she had once felt trapped here. The worn floors bore the scuffs of her restless pacing as a teenager, dreaming of escape. The faded floral wallpaper in the hallway still curled at the edges, neglected but stubbornly clinging on—like the town itself, refusing to change no matter how much time passed. Even her vanity, chipped at the corner and missing a brass pull, had belonged to her mother. She had once sworn she would leave this furniture, this town, this life, far behind her. Yet here she sat again, the glossy smear of lipstick on her lips like war paint.

Bitter thoughts occupied her mind.

She'd lied about her reasons for coming back. Lied to anyone who bothered to ask and, perhaps most importantly, lied to herself. The truth tasted too much like failure.

Back to this small town with its smaller people.

The words echoed inside her head with venom. They had never understood her, not really. These neighbors and classmates, these church ladies and softball players—they lived and breathed contentment, as though a porch swing and a family recipe could be enough to fill a life. To Briana, it had always been suffocating, as though someone pressed a pillow to her face every time she walked down Main Street.

They had no idea there was a wild, wonderful world beyond this sleepy place. A world that had welcomed her once.

She saw it again in her mind, clear as if it were yesterday: bright lights glinting off tall buildings, the rush of traffic and laughter spilling from rooftop bars, the feeling of possibility hanging in the air like perfume. There she had been someone. Beautiful, admired, unburdened by the old stories of who she used to be. She had slipped into that world like sliding into silk sheets. Effortless. Intoxicating.

Until she crashed.

Her hand hesitated as she painted the bow of her lip, the memory of that fall sharp as broken glass. She had flown too close to the sun, dazzled by her own reflection in windows and champagne flutes. She'd mistaken attention for devotion, mistook desire for permanence. And when it ended - when the city closed its doors to her - she found herself driving back to Tennessee, nursing wounds too deep for bandages.

Coming back to Pickwick Bend had been her only option.

She hated the sound of that, hated how it branded her return with desperation instead of choice. She told herself she had come back to take stock, to regroup, to remind herself of her roots. But really, she'd come back because there was nowhere else left to go.

And then, miracle of miracles, Acen had shown up in town shortly after she'd arrived.

She'd thought fate was smiling on her again.

For weeks she had floated on that possibility, certain the universe had realigned in her favor. The boy she had once known, now a man, returned at the very moment she needed a lifeline. She saw in him not just a chance at rekindling old sparks, but proof that she was still chosen, still worth fighting for. She had told herself stories of how it might unfold: the town buzzing with envy as they walked side by side, Acen's gaze fixed only on her, the life she'd once dreamed of finally within her reach.

But that hadn't turned out the way she'd thought.

Rose McAlister had ruined that dream.

Rose, with her polished little coffee shop and her air of calm competence, with her untouchable reputation and her easy way of making people like her. Rose, who had managed to turn Acen's head without even trying, while Briana had painted her nails and smiled too wide, offering everything and receiving nothing.

So now she'd get her own back the only way she could.

The thought curled in her chest like smoke. She leaned closer to the mirror, dragging the lipstick carefully along her bottom lip until it shone, until her reflection looked fierce enough to match the storm behind her eyes.

She didn't need to see the ripple to know it was there.

Small towns ran on gasoline and gossip, and she'd poured enough into the tank to keep tongues wagging for weeks.

The art of it, she told herself, was subtlety. You didn't shout the truth—or the lie. You whispered. You dropped a phrase here, an observation there. You looked surprised when someone else repeated it, and you tilted your head just enough to suggest you knew more than you were saying.

She didn't have to say the secret outright.

That was the beauty of it. She didn't have to spell out the details, didn't have to risk exposing herself to blame. She only had to tilt the story so it slid in Rose's direction. Just enough to remind people that Rose wasn't perfect, wasn't untouchable, wasn't the saint they wanted her to be.

And once the idea took root, it would grow.

That was the thing about suggestion. It bloomed wild, tangled, unstoppable. Like kudzu creeping up a fence post, once planted it covered everything in its path. She had already heard whispers of it—the way someone would lower their voice in the grocery aisle, the way a church pew would shift slightly when Rose sat down. Doubt was a seed you never had to water; people did it themselves.

Her reflection smirked back at her, lips red as sin, eyes narrowed with satisfaction. She leaned back, taking in the whole picture of herself in the mirror. She looked nothing like the girl who had once stared out this same window and dreamed of leaving. She looked harder, sharper, like someone who had survived too much to ever be soft again.

The house around her was still the same—thin walls, sagging roofline, the faint scent of mothballs in the closets. But she was not the same. She refused to be.

When the game ended. If she lost. If the town wanted to make her the villain, so be it. Villains got remembered.

She reached for the perfume bottle on her dresser, misting the air until the room filled with the sweet, heavy scent. She closed her eyes, breathing it in, letting the fragrance coat her skin like armor.

By the time she stood, smoothing down her skirt and slipping into her heels, the decision had already been made.

Rose McAlister might believe she had the upper hand. But Briana knew better.

Because in Pickwick Bend, it wasn't the truth that mattered.

It was the story people chose to believe.

And Briana Lewis knew exactly how to tell a story.

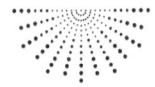

CHAPTER THIRTY-TWO

Rose couldn't ignore it anymore.

At the ball field, when she bent to tie her cleats, she caught two players on another team staring, whispering behind their hands. At the grocery store, Mrs. Lanham from down the street tilted her head in that pitying way that said she knew *something*. Even Riley noticed, slamming his hand on the counter at the coffee shop when a couple of men chuckled on their way out without explaining the joke.

"You want me to go after them?" Riley demanded.

Rose grabbed his arm before he could storm out. "No. That's exactly what Briana wants. She wants a show."

"Why not give her one?" Riley's voice dropped "This is killing me, Rose. Acen too. We're supposed to be protecting you. Standing up for you. This waiting game is crazy."

Rose didn't answer, but her silence was enough.

He swore under his breath, tugging his cap lower. "Then we need a plan. Because this town? They love a whisper. They'll build a mountain out of a pebble if you let 'em."

Rose nodded slowly, her chest tight. She'd fought hard to build a life that felt steady again. She wouldn't let Briana wreck it with shadows and half-truths.

But she also knew Briana.

And Briana wasn't done yet.

By Friday night, Rose could hardly breathe under the weight of it. The whispers felt like gnats. Small. Annoying. Impossible to swat away because as soon as she smacked one, three more rose up buzzing around her ears.

She told herself she was imagining it. That folks had always looked twice when she walked by because she ran the only coffee shop for twenty miles, and because she'd never exactly blended in with her wild red hair and tendency to speak her mind. But deep down, she knew.

Briana's fingerprints were all over this.

Tasha followed her into the stockroom after Cindy left for the day, arms crossed, her braid swinging against her shoulder. "You gonna tell me this isn't eating you alive? Are you gonna keep pretending you don't notice every time somebody looks sideways?"

Rose stacked sugar bags a little too hard. "Nothing's

eating me alive. Just stress. Tournament's this weekend. You know how I get."

"Mm-hm." Tasha didn't budge. "You also chew on your thumbnail when you're lying, and right now it looks like you're fixin' to gnaw it clean off."

Rose glanced down. Sure enough, her thumbnail was raw. She shoved both hands into her apron pockets. "I don't want to talk about it."

Tasha softened, stepping closer. "Rosie... I know Briana. And I know you. This has got her perfume all over it."

Rose's throat tightened. She wanted to laugh, wanted to shrug it off, but Tasha's eyes, the same steady gaze that had seen her through a hundred mistakes and a thousand heartbreaks, were too sharp, too knowing.

Finally, she whispered, "I'm making a plan. I'm not sure I can go through with it yet so I'm not gonna tell you what it is. Okay? And please don't mention it to Riley or Acen. I can't stand for them to pester me about what it is."

The look in Tasha's eyes said it was all she could do to nod her reluctant agreement.

That night, Rose couldn't sleep.

Her lake house felt darker than usual, shadows thick around the windows. She tossed and turned, memories swirling. Briana and Acen kissing on graduation night. Acen leaving town. Briana leaving town. Her secret dragging her down, down, down into a dark place she thought she'd never recover from.

Now, Briana was dragging her back there.

And Rose hated herself for letting it work.

But the fear in her chest felt exactly the same.

The silence pressed in on her. Out at the lake, nights could be achingly quiet, so quiet that the sound of water lapping at the rocks seemed louder than her own heartbeat. The old house creaked in its bones as if it, too, remembered what had once been buried here. She wrapped her arms around herself and stared at her reflection in the black kitchen window.

Her face looked older, wiser maybe, but the eyes staring back at her were too familiar. They were the eyes of the girl who had once cried herself to sleep, terrified that everyone would know her mistake, her weakness, her shame.

She had promised herself, back then, that she'd never give Briana the satisfaction of seeing her broken. Never again.

And yet, here she was, pacing the linoleum floor like a teenager waiting for the other shoe to drop.

She poured a glass of water just to keep her hands busy, then set it down untouched. The clock ticked past two-thirty. She thought about calling Tasha, just to hear another voice, but she didn't. Tasha would hear the wobble in her tone, would press her until she said more than she was ready to say.

Instead, she went to the porch and stepped into the night.

The air was damp, heavy with the scent of honeysuckle and lake water. A thin mist floated above the shoreline, wrapping the world in secrecy. She leaned against the porch rail and let the night press against her skin. Out here, away from town, she could almost believe the whispers didn't exist. Almost.

But her mind wouldn't let go.

She thought about the way Mrs. Lanham's eyes had softened in pity. The way those men had laughed at the coffee shop. The way the some of the people in town had nudged each other and smirked. Each glance, each whisper was like a drop of acid. It didn't destroy her all at once—it wore her down, slowly, carefully, until she was raw.

She remembered being eighteen, sneaking out to cry by the lake when it all got too heavy. She remembered the panic, the dread that the truth would spill out, that people would look at her differently forever. And here she was, twenty years later, still bracing herself for the same storm.

She gripped the rail until her knuckles turned white. "No," she said aloud, her voice swallowed by the night. "Not again."

Inside, she forced herself to sit at the table, pulled a notebook toward her, and opened it to a blank page. If she was going to get through this, she needed more than stubbornness. She needed to make a plan. The one she'd told Tasha earlier that she was already working on.

But staring at the empty paper, her mind refused to

cooperate. What could she write? That she'd expose Briana? That she'd confess her secret before Briana could use it? That she'd act like nothing mattered at all?

Every option felt like a trap.

Her pen hovered. Her hand trembled. She thought about Acen. His eyes when he'd told her he still cared, the way his presence stirred something she thought had long since burned out. She thought about Declan. Steady, gentle, showing her what it could feel like to be chosen without drama or conditions.

And she thought about Riley, protective as always, furious that he couldn't fix this for her.

For them, she had to be stronger.

She scribbled a single sentence across the page: *Briana does not get to win.*

The words steadied her.

It wasn't a plan, not yet, but it was a promise.

The clock chimed three. Her eyes burned from lack of sleep, but she felt a thread of steel slide through her spine. Briana wanted her rattled. She *wanted* Rose to look over her shoulder, to doubt herself, to break down in public so everyone could see.

But Rose refused to play the part Briana had written for her.

She tore the page free, folded it, and tucked it into the pocket of her robe. A talisman, small but fierce, something to hold onto when the whispers felt louder than the truth.

Finally, she turned off the lights, lay down on the

couch, and closed her eyes. Sleep came in fits and starts, tangled with dreams of softball fields, coffee cups, and shadows whispering her name.

And when dawn broke over the lake, painting the sky in streaks of pink and gold, Rose sat up with the sun on her face and whispered again, steady this time:

"I'm not eighteen anymore."

CHAPTER THIRTY-THREE

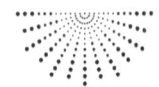

The rocking chair creaked beneath her as she leaned back, the sound a steady rhythm in the otherwise quiet house. The chair had belonged to her mother, one of the few pieces of furniture Briana had claimed when she returned to Pickwick Bend. The cushions were worn, faded to a pale rose color, with a faint smell of lavender clinging to the fabric. Her mother had always been proud of that scent, lavender sachets tucked into every drawer, sprigs tied with ribbon on the backs of chairs, oils dabbed at her wrists like perfume.

Now it clung to Briana like a ghost.

She hated that smell. It reminded her of a woman who'd stayed put, who'd never dared leave this town, who'd been content with smallness. And for years, Briana had told herself she would be different. She had been different. She had gotten out. She had gone places where no one knew her last name or cared about the McAllister twins or the softball championships at Pickwick High.

And yet—here she was again. Back in the same house. Back in the same town. Sitting in the same creaky chair her mother had rocked away her evenings in, staring down at a phone instead of a hymnbook.

The irony wasn't lost on her.

Her smirk faltered, just a touch, before she reapplied it like armor.

Because unlike her mother, Briana wasn't resigned to her fate. She still had fight left in her. She still had the ability to shape the story, to twist it, to make people look at Rose the way she wanted them to.

The whispers weren't just entertainment. They were power.

Briana crossed her legs, the hem of her silk robe sliding against her thigh as she set her phone on the side table. Her glass of wine caught the lamplight, rich red liquid glowing like blood in the cut-crystal goblet. She sipped it slowly, savoring the burn as it slipped down her throat.

Every whisper that spread through town was like that wine—warm, intoxicating, filling her up in ways she hadn't felt in years.

Rose, perfect Rose, with her clean little coffee shop and her neat little softball team, pretending she was the queen of Pickwick Bend.

It made Briana's teeth ache just thinking about it.

She remembered those days in high school, how Rose had been the golden one. Always steady, always dependable, always liked. Teachers praised her, boys orbited her, even Acen - back then, the boy everyone wanted - had looked at her with eyes that Briana had wanted for herself.

Briana had learned then that admiration was a form of currency in this town. And she'd spent twenty years trying to prove she could buy more than Rose ever could. She had gone out, she had lived, she had *escaped.*

But when she fell—when the money dried up, when the doors closed, when the people who had once clapped for her stopped answering her calls where had she ended up?

Right back where she started.

Back in the rocking chair.

Back under her mother's roof, though her mother was long gone.

The humiliation of that burned deeper than anything Rose could ever say or do.

Which was why Rose had to fall too.

Briana tilted her head, watching her reflection in the darkened window across the room. Her face was still beautiful. High cheekbones, glossy hair, lips painted the perfect shade of red. But beneath it, she could see the shadows. The fine lines where laughter had been replaced with calculation. The slight hollowness at her cheeks that no amount of makeup could fully disguise.

She leaned forward, resting her elbows on her knees, letting the rocking chair sway with her movement.

She whispered it aloud, just to taste the words in the air.

"They'll eat her alive."

It was true. This town didn't need proof. They needed suggestion. They needed the spark of an idea, and then they would fan it into a blaze with their own breath. That was how small towns worked. Nobody admitted to loving gossip, but everybody did. It was the currency, the entertainment, the lifeblood.

And Rose's life was ripe for it.

Briana didn't have to lie. She didn't even have to push too hard. All she had to do was tilt her head, smile faintly, and let her words trail off in the right direction.

"Bless her heart."

That was enough.

Because *bless her heart* was Southern for *wait until you hear this.*

Her phone buzzed again, the screen lighting up with another message. This one wasn't a question. It was a statement.

"Never thought she'd let something like that happen."

Briana's smile sharpened as she typed back: *"Me neither."*

Send.

It was almost too easy.

She leaned back again, the chair groaning in

protest. For a moment, she closed her eyes, letting the rhythm of the rocking soothe her. She could almost imagine her mother sitting there, humming softly, hands folded in her lap. But Briana wasn't humming hymns. She was orchestrating downfall.

And the sweetest part?

She didn't even have to lie.

Rose had given her the truth years ago, whether she knew it or not.

Briana had just been smart enough to keep it tucked away, waiting for the day it might serve her. Oh, she had enjoyed scaring Rose back in those days. Letting Rose think she was going to tell the whole town her precious little secret. But, even then, she'd known this secret might be an ace up her sleeve someday. And how right she'd been to keep it carefully tucked away until the right time.

That day had arrived.

The night deepened around her. Outside, cicadas buzzed, a low, pulsing song. The air was heavy, thick with June heat, pressing against the windows. Briana's skin prickled with it, but she didn't move to open a window. She liked the closeness, the way it mirrored the pressure she was applying to Rose's world.

Slow. Suffocating. Inescapable.

She sipped her wine again, lips curving against the glass.

CHAPTER THIRTY-FOUR

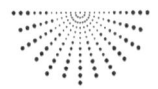

Saturday morning dawned too bright. Semi-finals day.

The softball field was already buzzing by the time Rose pulled her truck into the gravel lot. Heat shimmered above the fields though the sun hadn't yet reached its peak.

Families hauled coolers and umbrellas across the grass, folding chairs slung over shoulders. The smell of grilled hot dogs drifted from the concession stand, mingling with sunscreen and the metallic tang of red dust kicked up by sneakers.

Kids darted across the outfield chasing foul balls, their laughter carrying high and shrill over the low hum of voices. The bleachers creaked and groaned as neighbors settled in for a long day of games, settling themselves like birds lining a fence.

Rose should've felt at home here. She'd been

playing since she was a teenager, and coaching now gave her the same rush she used to feel rounding third with the crowd roaring. The rhythm of the sport had always steadied her, rooted her, given her something she could count on. But today, as she adjusted her cap and gathered the girls, the stares hit her like pitches to the ribs.

"Eyes on me!" she barked, forcing her voice steady as she walked the lineup through their warmups.

The girls obeyed with enthusiasm, ponytails bobbing as they jogged through drills. Gloves snapped open and shut. Bats cracked against soft tosses, echoing like distant firecrackers. Their cheers rang loud, oblivious to the undercurrents twisting through the stands.

But Tasha wasn't fooled. She sat on the bench, water bottle tucked between her knees, eyes narrowing as she caught the flicker of panic in Rose's gaze. Her friend's smile didn't quite reach her eyes.

She nudged Acen, who leaned against the dugout rail with his arms crossed, posture loose but eyes sharp.

"She's rattled," Tasha murmured.

Acen frowned, the crease deepening between his brows. "Yeah. I see it."

He'd been watching Rose all morning. How her shoulders hunched tighter than usual, how she avoided looking at the crowd, how she snapped at Riley for forgetting the batting order.

Rose clapped her hands, trying to infuse energy

into her voice. "Let's go, ladies! Semi-final starts in ten —let's make it count!"

The girls cheered, but Rose's throat burned.

The first inning went smoothly enough. Rose kept her eyes trained on the field, calling signals, clapping encouragement, reminding herself that the game was all that mattered. Her girls hustled, snagging line drives, sliding into bases, chalk dust flying.

But in the stands, whispers began to stir like wind through dry grass.

Marlene sat in the second row with her church friends, a wide-brimmed hat shading her eyes. She leaned in, lowering her voice to just the right pitch. Quiet enough to sound conspiratorial, loud enough to ensure the row behind her would catch every word.

"I heard it from someone who'd know," she said, her lips pursed with reluctant authority.

Her friend's eyes widened. "No..."

"Well, I don't know for sure," Marlene went on, feigning reluctance, "but doesn't it make you wonder?"

Another woman in a visor clucked her tongue. "You never can tell about people."

Gasps and murmurs rippled outward, subtle but steady, like a pebble tossed into a still pond. Heads bent together. Eyebrows raised. A few hands covered mouths, though smiles tugged at the corners.

Rose could feel it, even from the dugout. The weight of their stares pressed between her shoulder blades, heavy as cinder blocks. Every time she walked toward third base to wave a runner home, she felt eyes pinning her like butterflies to corkboard.

The second inning cracked open with tension. One of her girls, Maggie popped a fly ball into shallow right. The outfielder sprinted forward, glove snapping shut just as Maggie's cleats hit the bag at first base.

"Dang it!" Rose clapped her hands, loud and encouraging, masking her own fray of nerves. "Shake it off, Maggie! We'll get the next one!"

The girls echoed her, chanting their teammate's name. But Rose's palms sweated around the clipboard. She shifted it against her hip, the metal clip biting into her side. Her eyes darted once toward the stands and immediately wished they hadn't.

A group of mothers in lawn chairs turned their heads in unison, lips moving, eyes glittering with curiosity. When Rose's gaze caught theirs, they didn't look away. They smiled too sweetly, the way one might smile at someone you pitied.

Her throat tightened.

"Coach?" Acen's voice cut through her haze.

She blinked, jerking her attention back to the game. Acen was holding up the lineup card, confusion written across his face. "Who's on deck? You skipped."

Rose swallowed hard. "Uh—Jessie. Jessie's up."

Her voice cracked just enough for Acen to notice. He caught Riley's frown from his position behind the backstop and stepped closer to Rose.

Between innings, he finally pulled her aside, hand light on her elbow. "What's going on?"

"Nothing." She reached for the clipboard like it was a shield, clutching it against her chest.

"Rose. Don't let her get to you." His voice softened, but his eyes were steady, insistent. "Talk to me."

Her pulse stuttered under the intensity of his gaze.

"Focus on the game," she said briskly, forcing her tone back to business. She turned, walking toward the dugout before he could press further.

Acen let her go, jaw tightening. He wasn't done.

By mid-afternoon, the gossip had matured into something sturdier than whispers.

"That's what I heard too," a man in a Memphis Tigers cap said from the top row.

His wife shook her head. "Mercy, if it's true…"

"Well," Marlene chimed in again, voice sweet as syrup, "I just pray for her. That's all you can do, isn't it? Pray."

But her eyes glittered beneath the brim of her hat.

Another woman leaned closer. "Makes sense, though. Explains why she never—"

Rose couldn't hear the rest, but she didn't need to. She could feel it in the way their voices cut off when she glanced their way. In the too-casual way someone laughed too loudly at nothing.

Her team clapped and stomped as they scored a run, cheers echoing across the field. Rose forced a smile, but inside she wanted to scream. She wanted to whirl on the bleachers and shout, *Mind your business! Keep your poison to yourself!* She wanted to march up to Briana wherever she was hiding herself today - because of course Briana was the source - and demand she rot in her bitterness.

But her girls were watching. And Rose had always promised herself she'd be better than the people who'd torn her down.

So she clapped harder. Louder. Until her palms stung.

The game stretched long, every inning sticky with tension. Rose coached like a woman at war with herself. Her voice firm, her face impassive, but her body taut as a drawn bow. Every call, every substitution, every clap of encouragement felt like an act of defiance.

By the seventh inning, her team had edged out a narrow lead. The final out came on a strike, the opposing batter's shoulders slumping as the umpire called it. The girls erupted into cheers, dogpiling near the mound, dust rising in a golden cloud.

Rose clapped, shouting encouragement, but she felt hollow. The victory didn't settle inside her the way it used to. The girls hugged and laughed, but Rose's gaze kept flicking back to the bleachers, to the clusters of neighbors still murmuring as they gathered their things.

After the game, the field began to empty. Folding chairs folded. Coolers rattled back to trucks. The sun dipped lower, baking the dust into reddish crust beneath their shoes.

Rose lingered by the dugout, clipboard limp in her hand. She wanted to go home, to shut the door, to be anywhere but under the weight of all those eyes.

But as she rounded the corner of the concession stand, Declan was waiting.

His ball cap shaded his steady gaze, and his arms hung loose at his sides. He wasn't smiling, but there was no judgment in his face either. Just quiet steadiness.

"You okay?" he asked.

The words were simple, but they cracked something inside her. She opened her mouth to say yes, but the word caught in her throat.

Instead, she looked past him toward the field, now nearly empty, dust swirling in lazy eddies. "Just tired."

Declan didn't push. He just nodded, the silence stretching comfortable, steady. He stood there with her, quiet and unshakable, like he was giving her the space to climb down from the wall she'd built, brick by trembling brick.

CHAPTER THIRTY-FIVE

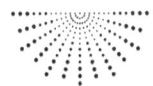

That evening, Briana poured another glass of wine and sat by her window, enjoying the faint breeze stirring the curtains. She hummed, content. The game had been a perfect stage. The whispers were stronger now, loud enough to sting but soft enough that Rose couldn't fight back without naming the very thing she wanted hidden.

It was working.

But Briana wasn't finished.

She pulled a notepad from her purse and jotted down a few lines, testing the shape of them. An anonymous note, just vague enough to plant deeper suspicion. Something that could slip under a coffee shop door, or appear in a church pew, or get tucked into the box of pies at the farmers market.

A secret wasn't truly power until it was dangled just out of reach.

And Briana intended to dangle it until Rose broke.

CHAPTER THIRTY-SIX

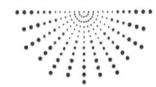

M onday started with silence.

Not the peaceful kind. Not the early-morning quiet Rose usually cherished when opening the coffee shop. This was a different kind of silence. Sharp, expectant. The kind that hung in the air when someone had just walked into a room and no one wanted to be the one to say something first.

By ten a.m., she'd had three customers cancel pre-orders.

By noon, Mrs. Trammell, one of her steadiest regulars, walked past the window without coming inside for her usual latte.

Rose didn't need a town crier to know what was happening.

Briana had planted her seeds.

And now, like poison ivy, they were winding their way through Pickwick Bend.

She slammed a tray of muffins into the oven with a little more force than necessary.

"Need help with those or just working on your pitching arm?" came a voice from behind her.

She turned to see Acen standing in the doorway and wearing that maddeningly calm expression that always made her want to either kiss him or throw something.

Maybe both.

"I'm fine," she said.

"You're furious."

"I'm *focused.* There's a difference."

He stepped inside, sat on a stool at the counter. "Focused on what?"

"Keeping my business from collapsing."

He didn't reply right away. Just watched her as she paced her brow furrowed in frustration.

She slammed her hand on the wooden counter. "I thought people knew me better than this."

"They *do.* But gossip doesn't care about truth, and Briana's a master manipulator. If she can't destroy you head-on, she'll try to make people *question* you."

"Well, it's working."

He stepped closer. "So let's fight back."

Her arms crossed. "With what? Flyers? A press release? I'm not a politician."

"No," he said. "You're a business owner. A community staple. And you've got more support than you think."

Rose raised an eyebrow. "From who?"

He pulled a folded paper from his jacket and handed it to her.

She opened it to find a flyer mock-up: *Community Appreciation Night*—free samples, softball scrimmage, and a chance to support the coffee shop.

"You made this?"

"Cindy and Tasha helped," he said. "Riley's on board, and all of your rec league girls said they'd organize the game. You're the heart of this town, Rose. Briana's just noise."

Her throat tightened.

"Did someone tell the whole team my secret?" She asked, angry.

"Of course not." Acen brushed her hair back from her face. "But they aren't stupid, Rose. They know something's up. They've been your friends and on your team for years. They'd understand if you told them."

"You mean like the rest of the people in the town where I've spent my whole life are understanding?" She challenged.

Acen pulled her into his arms. "Rose. Not everyone is whispering about you. I know that's hard to believe right now. But there are just as many people who don't listen to those rumors as there are talking about them."

He handed her the mock flyer. "Let's do this. It will help. I promise."

"This is... a lot," she whispered.

"It's exactly what you deserve," Acen said. "To be lifted up. Not just defended, but *celebrated.*"

She stared at the flyer, the knot in her chest loosening for the first time all day.

"What if it backfires?" she asked. "What if people don't show up?"

"Then we eat the cupcakes ourselves," he said with a grin. "But they *will* show up. Because you've fed them, coached them, donated to their fundraisers, and remembered their birthdays with extra muffins."

She looked up at him.

"I don't want to do this alone," she said.

"You're not," he replied. "Not anymore."

That night, Rose sat with Tasha and Cindy at Cindy's kitchen table, planning the event.

Tasha handled the community outreach. "I'll post on social media, and I'll talk to Marcy at the PTA. We'll call it something catchy. 'Curveballs and Cupcakes' or 'Sweet Revenge.'"

Cindy snorted. "How about 'Baked Goods and Bad Blood'?"

Rose laughed, really laughed, for the first time in days.

"Whatever we call it," she said, "we do it on the field. I want people to *see* who I am. Not just a name in a rumor."

Tasha nodded. "You've got the team behind you."

Cindy raised her glass of sweet tea. "To the comeback of the year."

And as the night went on, the plans grew.

Flyers. Cupcake flavors. A playlist. A silent auction for charity. Even a dunk tank. Tasha's idea, naturally, with her name first on the seat.

Rose watched her friends, her heart swelling.

She'd spent years believing her story ended in heartbreak.

But maybe it was just a long, winding inning.

And she was finally stepping up to bat.

CHAPTER THIRTY-SEVEN

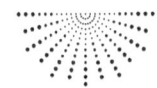

By Wednesday morning, the buzz in Pickwick Bend was undeniable.

Flyers for *"Baked & Bold: A Sweet Night for Pickwick Bend"* were taped to shop windows, pinned to bulletin boards at the rec center, and stacked neatly in piles at the coffee shop's front counter. The event would include free dessert samples, a charity softball game featuring the women's team, and a live auction with donations from nearly every local business.

Rose was trying not to get her hopes up.

But when Mrs. Trammell showed up just after the coffee shop opened, holding a flyer and ordering not one, but two chocolate muffins, her heart gave a little kick.

Still, she wasn't naïve.

She knew Briana wasn't finished.

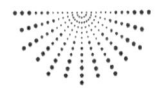

CHAPTER THIRTY-EIGHT

Briana stood in front of Declan's vet office, her phone pressed to her ear, watching as customers strolled in and out with curious glances. She'd noticed the change too—more people smiling at Rose, more backing away from whispers. The tide was turning.

And that terrified her.

She'd felt in control, tugging strings, sowing doubt like seed scattered on dry ground. And at first, it had sprouted beautifully. Sideways looks, whispered questions, Rose flinching like she'd been caught doing something wrong. That was what Briana lived for, the satisfaction of knowing Rose couldn't walk ten feet without wondering who was talking about her.

But now? The threads were loosening. Folks were circling back to Rose, smiling in her direction, choosing to see her coffee shop as the heart of the town again instead of the scandal Briana hinted at. It made Briana's jaw clench. Nothing slipped through her fingers without a fight.

So she dialed the number she'd been avoiding.

When the line clicked, she smiled.

"Hi, Richard," she purred, her voice low, syrupy. "It's Briana. I know it's been a long time, but I have a story you might want to print."

The name rolled off her tongue with practiced ease. Richard wasn't just any reporter. He was the type who thrived on town drama, who lived to splash ink across paper that would sit on church pews, diner counters, and gas station shelves by morning. She'd given him tips before, years ago, and he'd eaten them up like a starving dog.

Briana stepped away from the window and into the shadow of the alley, her heels clicking against the pavement before she stopped. The air smelled faintly of feed and antiseptic drifting from the clinic. She leaned against the brick wall, her tone dropping into a practiced sort of sweet venom.

"It's about Rose McAllister. And that coffee shop she runs? Well, let's just say it's not the sugar-sweet picture everyone thinks. She's throwing a charity event, but what if it's really about saving face after a scandal? There's a lot people don't know. About her, about her past with Acen Wheeler. Doesn't that seem… newsworthy?"

She let the silence on the other end stretch; her own

reflection caught faintly in the clinic's darkened glass. Her smile grew sharper. Richard didn't need much convincing; she could already hear the scratching of his pen in her imagination, could almost see the bold headline.

Her stomach fluttered, equal parts nerves and thrill. This was better than whispers. This was permanence. Print lasted. People clipped articles, tucked them into Bibles, folded them into drawers, carried them like proof.

She paused, then smiled again, pushing sweetness into her voice like cream into bitter coffee.

"Oh, I can get you records. Copies of her old messages. I'm sure someone kept them."

It was a lie, but a beautiful one, and lies had always served her well. Truth was messy, unpredictable. Lies, however, were art. She could paint them however she wanted, and people would stand back and admire the brushstrokes without ever asking to see the canvas up close.

Her thumb toyed with the edge of her phone as she leaned harder against the wall, heart thrumming. Rose had always been the golden girl, even after being knocked down. Folks liked to root for her, to pretend her scars made her stronger. It was nauseating.

What they didn't understand. What they refused to understand. Was that Rose's survival came at Briana's expense. Rose's strength was always built from the rubble Briana had been buried under. Perfect Rose from the perfect family. While Briana had struggled in poverty all her growing up years. Trying harder than anyone else to be someone. And Rose. Always Rose beating her in everything. It sickened her to remember the years that she had pretended to be Rose's friend to get close to everyone else.

Well, no more.

If the town wouldn't listen to her in whispers, maybe they'd believe it in print.

She closed her eyes for a beat, inhaling the dampness of the shaded alley, letting her heartbeat slow. A single article could undo everything Rose had built. People wouldn't look at her coffee shop with the same warmth anymore. They'd walk in hesitantly, whispering behind menus, wondering if their lattes were being served with a side of shame. They'd avoid her eyes at church, tilt their heads with that familiar pity, that smug satisfaction that said *we knew she wasn't perfect.*

Briana fed on that kind of shift. It wasn't enough to win; she needed Rose to lose. Needed her to feel that hollow ache of being left out, looked down on, whispered about.

Her mind darted back to high school, the nights when she and Rose were inseparable, when secrets were shared on quilts in Rose's room under a ceiling fan that clicked with every turn. Back then, Rose had trusted her. Back then, Rose had loved her like a sister.

And then Acen.

Always Acen.

Briana swallowed hard, heat rising behind her ribs. He had been hers first. Her hand to hold, her name whispered into the night. But somehow, Rose had always been between them. Her laugh too loud, her eyes too bright, her presence impossible to ignore. And when Acen finally chose? When he finally turned away?

That wound never healed.

Every rumor Briana started, every whisper she nurtured, was just another stitch in the tapestry she'd been weaving. A picture where Rose wasn't the darling of Pickwick Bend anymore.

She slipped her phone back into her purse and straightened, brushing invisible lint from her blouse. Her smirk lingered.

This was just the beginning.

Because once words were printed, they couldn't be taken back.

And when the town of Pickwick Bend read her story, Briana knew one thing for certain: Rose McAllister wouldn't be able to walk down Main Street without feeling the weight of every eye.

Exactly the way Briana wanted it.

CHAPTER THIRTY-NINE

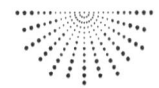

T he next morning, Rose stepped out to grab the newspaper from the rack outside the coffee shop - and froze.

There, below the fold of the Pickwick Gazette, was a headline in bold:

"Sweet Lies? Local Barista's Past Stirring Up Small-Town Drama"

And beneath it, a grainy photo of Rose, cropped from a festival booth five years ago, her smile wide, her hands holding two large coffees.

She flipped the page with numb fingers.

There it was—just enough truth to be dangerous, just enough speculation to light a match.

A "source close to the situation" mentioned a teenage romance gone wrong and a bitter rift between former best friends. It was exactly the kind of thing

Pickwick Bend pretended not to care about. While eating it up with a spoon.

Behind her, the coffee shop door opened.

"Rose?" Tasha's voice. "You okay?"

She turned, holding up the paper.

And for the first time in days, she didn't feel anger.

She felt done.

Done hiding. Done reacting. Done letting Briana shape her story.

"This ends now," she said, her voice steady.

"I'm going to tell them everything."

The sun dipped low over Pickwick Lake, casting a warm glow over the ballfield as the sound of laughter and chatter drifted on the breeze. Kids dashed between folding tables, faces sticky with frosting. Neighbors passed around platters of cupcakes, peach cobbler, and slices of strawberry cake with hand-lettered signs reading *"Baked with Love by Rose."*

The stands were full.

The team was in uniform.

And Rose wasn't trying to blend in.

She was trying to *be seen.*

Tasha grabbed her hand as they stood near the bleachers. "You sure about this?"

Rose nodded, her heart pounding but steady. "If I don't tell it, Briana will keep rewriting it for me."

Cindy appeared with a cordless microphone and a wink. "Time to break the curse, Cinderella."

Rose laughed nervously, then climbed the small set of stairs onto the makeshift stage they'd built from the high school's band risers. The music faded. The crowd quieted.

She looked out across the field—the bleachers, the lawn chairs, the people who'd bought her muffins and watched her grow up and spread rumors about her and shown up tonight anyway.

Acen stood near the dugout, arms folded, expression open and unwavering.

Riley gave her a thumbs-up from behind home plate, where he was chasing off two toddlers using baseball gloves as hats.

Rose took a breath. And then she spoke.

"I don't really like microphones," she said, earning a few chuckles. "Or being the center of attention. Which is funny, considering how many people have had opinions about me lately."

That got more laughs—sharper ones.

"I read the article," she said plainly. "And I'm not here to refute it or spin it. I'm just here to tell the truth."

The crowd leaned in.

"I was eighteen when I fell in love with Acen Wheeler. He was my brother's best friend, and we were young and messy and full of hope. I thought we had forever. But forever didn't come. And when it ended, it didn't just break my heart. It broke part of me."

The field was quiet now. Still.

"After he left town, I found out I was pregnant. I didn't tell anyone. Not even him. And before I could figure out how to deal with it, I lost the baby. I thought I was being punished for something. I thought it was my fault. And instead of facing it, I shut down."

A sharp breath rippled through the crowd. But no one left.

"I spent years letting that secret fester. Letting someone else, someone I once trusted, hold it over me. But I'm done with that. I'm done being ashamed of what happened to me. I'm done pretending I'm someone I'm not."

She looked around at the people gathered.

"I'm Rose McAllister. I'm not perfect. I've made mistakes. But I've also baked your birthday cakes, and coached your kids, and stayed in this town because I love it. Because it's *my* town, too. And I won't let anyone shame me out of it again."

Applause started on the left side of the bleachers, slow but strong.

Then it grew.

Until the whole crowd was on their feet.

Cheering.

Clapping.

Whistling.

Even a few tears.

Rose blinked hard, smiling despite the tears pricking her eyes.

When the noise finally settled, she added with a shaky laugh, "Now if you'll excuse me, I've got a game to play and a team to coach."

Cheers followed her as she stepped down, her knees weak, her hands trembling but her heart *clear.*

Acen met her at the bottom of the stairs.

"You were incredible," he said.

"I was terrified."

"That's what makes it brave."

She looked up at him. "It doesn't fix everything."

"No," he said. "But it starts something new."

He held out his hand.

She took it.

Behind them, the lights flickered on over the field.

The game was about to begin.

CHAPTER FORTY

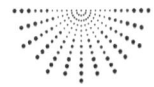

The field was alive with energy.

Rose stood on first base, her glove in hand, her cleats planted in the worn red clay. The bleachers were packed, the lights buzzing overhead, and laughter drifted from the concession table where kids clutched frosted cupcakes and drippy popsicles.

"Alright, ladies," Tasha hollered from the pitcher's mound. "Let's show 'em how slow pitch is done. With style, sass, and a little scandal."

Laughter rippled through the infield.

Dani smirked from shortstop. "Speak for yourself. I'm just here for the post-game margaritas."

Rose grinned, relaxed for the first time in weeks.

The umpire, Mr. Caldwell from the bait shop, lifted his hand. "Batter up!"

They were playing against a co-ed team from the

firehouse, but tonight wasn't about winning. It was about showing up. For each other. For the town. For Rose.

Still, Rose fielded the first hit like a pro, scooping the ball and tagging first with a satisfying *thwack*.

Cheers erupted from the stands.

She turned and met Riley's eyes—he was standing behind the backstop fence and beaming like the proud twin brother he was. He tipped his cap dramatically, and she gave him a mock curtsey.

The next few innings flew by.

Tasha struck out two with her lethal underhand spin. Maggie made a behind-the-back catch that had the bleachers gasping. Even little Josie, who'd never played a sport before this season, caught a fly ball in right field.

And Rose?

She played like her life wasn't under scrutiny anymore.

She played like she belonged.

Because she did.

On the sidelines, Briana leaned against the fence, arms crossed, watching the game unfold with a tight jaw.

It hadn't gone as planned.

The article hadn't destroyed Rose. It had galvanized her. Given her a platform. And worse, given her the town's sympathy.

Even Declan hadn't returned her calls after it ran.

She turned to leave, heels crunching on gravel but stopped when she saw Mrs. Trammell block her path.

"Leaving so soon?" the older woman asked, arms folded in that knowing way of Southern women who've lived through everything twice.

Briana offered a strained smile. "I have somewhere to be."

"Mm-hmm," Mrs. Trammell said. "Seems to me you had something to prove tonight. Funny how it's Rose on the field, and you on the outside."

Briana didn't answer.

She didn't need to.

Because the truth was, everyone *had* picked a side.

And it wasn't hers.

Back on the field, the final inning was underway. Rose stepped up to the plate, bat in hand, heart steady.

The crowd quieted slightly.

Tasha shouted from the dugout, "Send that ball back to Memphis!"

Rose smirked.

Aunt Jean stood in the stands "Give 'em hell, Rosie!"

She squared her stance. The pitch came in, slow, high, looping and she swung.

Crack.

The ball sailed over second base, arcing perfectly into center field.

She ran to first, then second, her legs pumping, her breath sharp with joy.

The throw came in wild, and she saw Acen behind the backstop fence waving her around third and shouting, "GO, GO, GO!"

She slid into home plate in a cloud of dust and laughter, safe by a mile.

The crowd exploded.

And Rose, grinning, looked up at the stars above the field lights and felt something deep inside her settle.

Not just closure.

Peace.

After the game, the crowd lingered, music playing from the portable speaker Riley had somehow ducttaped to the backstop. Kids danced. Adults sipped sweet tea from plastic cups. And Rose stood near the cupcake table, handing out napkins and thank-yous.

Acen found her there, his shirt dusty, his eyes warm.

"You know you stole the show tonight, right?"

She handed him a mini lemon cupcake. "Think the town's forgiven me?"

"Forgiven you?" he said. "They *celebrated* you."

She looked out over the field, the lights, the laughter, the fading daylight.

"They didn't have to."

"No," he said. "But they wanted to."

He took a bite of the cupcake and added, mouth full, "Besides, you had 'em at free baked goods."

She laughed and leaned into him, her shoulder

brushing his. "You think this is it? That it's finally over?"

He looked down at her. "I think this is the beginning."

She nodded, the soft hum of contentment in her chest growing louder.

"Then let's see where it goes."

CHAPTER FORTY-ONE

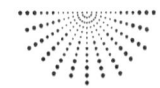

The morning after the charity event, the town felt hushed, as if it too were catching its breath.

Pickwick Bend had shown up and shown *out*. And Rose's inbox was full of messages from neighbors, classmates, even a couple of church ladies who'd recently given her the side-eye in Piggly Wiggly.

She should've been celebrating.

But something still pulled at her.

Declan.

Her heart ached when she thought of him. His kind eyes and patient words. The way he'd stepped close but never pushed. He'd offered steadiness when she'd been spinning, and she had clung to it longer than she should've. Longer than was fair.

She owed him honesty.

So that afternoon, she tied her apron strings in a

neat bow and twisted her hair into a lazy knot. She left the coffee shop as it hummed along under Cindy's capable hands, and she walked the few blocks to the vet office.

The late sunlight was soft, slanting gold across storefronts and making the brick buildings glow. The bell over the clinic door jingled when she pushed it open, and the scent of disinfectant and dog biscuits hit her all at once.

Declan looked up from behind the counter, where he was shuffling files into neat piles. He wore that same calm expression she'd come to know. The one that said nothing ruffled him for long. His smile was gentle, unguarded.

"Hey, Rose," he said. "I figured I might see you."

Her throat tightened, but she forced a small smile. "Can we talk?"

"Of course." He set the files down, folding his arms on the counter like he had all the time in the world.

She leaned against the edge of it, fiddling with the edge of her apron string. Her pulse thumped in her ears, loud enough she swore he could hear it.

"I owe you an apology," she began, words catching on her tongue. "For letting things go as far as they did when I wasn't sure I could return your feelings."

Declan tilted his head, his mouth curving just slightly.

"I always knew."

Her brows lifted. "You did?"

"I'm a good reader of people," he said with a half-smile. "Comes with being a veterinarian. You learn how to tell what's real and what's just been polished up."

The truth of it hit her like a pebble to glass. Rose's breath caught, guilt pricking her chest.

"I never wanted to hurt you," she whispered.

"You didn't." His voice was steady, almost tender. "You've got a big heart, Rose. It's just… not mine to hold."

The words loosened something inside her, and tears stung unexpectedly at the corners of her eyes. She blinked fast, refusing to let them fall. "You deserve someone who sees you first. Not as a distraction, or a safe option, but as the real thing."

"I know." He nodded slowly, the softest smile tugging at his lips. "And I'll find her. But I'm still glad I met you."

Her chest squeezed. Relief and sorrow tangled together, making it hard to breathe. She reached across the counter, sliding her hand into his. His palm was warm, callused, familiar.

"Me too," she said, and meant it.

For a long moment, they stood in that quiet, their hands joined, not as almost-somethings but as friends. Genuinely. Finally. The air between them felt different now, lighter, freed from all the weight of expectation.

Rose eased her hand back, though the warmth lingered. She thought of how easy it could've been to pretend, to let things continue as they had, to blur the lines and call it enough. But Declan deserved more than half-truths. And she did too.

"I need to get back to the coffee shop."

"That reminds me," Declan said as she straightened to leave, his tone shifting like sunlight breaking through clouds, "I've got a vintage rolling pin from the 1940s for you. Real maple. I found it at an antique store. Might come in handy if you ever need to beat off a jealous rival with style."

Rose blinked, then snorted. "Let's hope it doesn't come to that."

But the laugh that bubbled up surprised her—light, real, almost giddy. It shook loose some of the heaviness she'd been carrying.

As she stepped outside, the bell above the door chimed again, and she paused on the sidewalk. The air smelled of freshly cut grass and honeysuckle, warm against her skin. Across the street, kids were tossing a baseball back and forth, their shouts echoing off the buildings. Life went on, steady and sure.

She pressed a hand to her chest, exhaling slowly. Something inside her had shifted. She hadn't won or lost. She hadn't hurt Declan, nor had he hurt her. They had met in the middle, in the place where truth was softer but stronger than any illusion.

That evening, Rose stepped out the back door of the coffee shop and found Briana leaning against her truck.

Dressed in heels, oversized sunglasses, and spite.

"Didn't think you had the nerve to face me again," Rose said.

"I'm leaving town," Briana announced, arms folded. "For good this time. Thought you'd want to hear it from me."

Rose raised a brow. "And?"

"And I came to say congratulations."

It was flat, forced.

"And to let you know," Briana added, voice slipping toward venom, "that one day he'll leave again. Just like last time. You may have won the town, but people don't really change, Rose."

"Maybe not," Rose said calmly. "But I have. I don't need to win anymore. I just need to live honestly. Something you might try sometime."

Briana sneered. "You always did like the moral high ground."

"No," Rose said, opening her car door. "But it turns out, it has better views."

She climbed in and shut the door, leaving Briana standing there in her designer shoes and shrinking pride.

CHAPTER FORTY-TWO

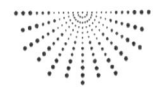

Rose found Acen waiting on her porch with two sweating glasses of sweet tea.

The sight stopped her in her tracks.

He sat on the top step like he belonged there, elbows balanced on his knees, the glasses catching the last shimmers of sunlight. Condensation pooled in rings on the porch rail where the glasses sat.

"I figured after the week you've had you might want some quiet," he said, offering her the glass.

She smiled, heart swelling at how well he knew her. Not just the outer version of her, the woman who plastered on a brave face for the town, who kept her shop running and her chin high. No, he knew the Rose who craved stillness after the storm, who found healing in silence and a glass of sweet tea on a porch swing.

"Quiet sounds about right," she said softly.

He rose easily, handing her one of the glasses, and

the cool condensation pressed against her palm as welcome as a blessing. They moved together toward the porch swing, falling into step like they'd been doing it for years.

The chains creaked as they settled onto the wooden slats, and the swing swayed gently beneath their weight.

The evening sky was painted lavender, streaks of rose and indigo stretching across the horizon. Honeysuckle curled along the fence line, its sweetness drifting on the breeze. The air held that soft heaviness particular to southern summers—the kind that wrapped around you like a quilt, both comfort and weight at once.

Rose took a sip of tea, the hint of lemon sharp and soothing all at once. She felt her heartbeat begin to slow, the day's ache loosening in her chest.

"Declan and I talked," she said, breaking the hush.

Acen didn't flinch, didn't bristle. He simply turned his head, one brow lifting slightly. "I figured. Everything okay?"

"Better than okay." She wrapped her fingers tight around the glass, condensation dripping onto her jeans. "He's a good man. Just not my man."

The relief of saying it aloud surprised her. She hadn't realized how much she'd carried until the words fell free.

Acen leaned back, his shoulder brushing hers as the swing rocked. He gazed at the tree branches, their leaves rustling in the evening breeze. His profile caught the fading light. Strong, steady, softened by something she couldn't name.

"I've been thinking," he said slowly. "About staying."

She turned to him, startled. The word *staying* rang in her chest like a church bell.

"You'd stay? Really stay?"

He set his glass down on the rail beside the swing and laced his fingers together, as if steadying himself for the truth. "I got an offer to coach the high school's boys' baseball team. It's not glamorous. But it's steady. And it'd mean I'm not just… passing through again."

Rose felt her throat tighten. She stared at him, her glass forgotten. Memories tumbled through her mind. The boy who left, the man who'd walked back into her life, the years she'd spent convincing herself she was fine without him.

And here he was, offering something she had secretly longed for but never dared hope.

He looked at her then, steady and sure, no trace of hesitation in his eyes. "I've spent enough years running. If I'm going to plant roots again, I want to do it beside someone who makes me feel like home."

Her breath hitched.

That word. *Home.*

It wasn't about houses or towns. It was about belonging. About being seen and chosen, not in spite of scars but because of them.

A slow smile broke across her face before she even

realized it, her chest filling with a warmth that felt like sunlight after a long winter.

And then, before she could say a word, he kissed her.

It wasn't rushed or fiery. It was careful. Certain.

A kiss twenty years in the making, and worth every lost second.

Her heart galloped as his lips pressed against hers, gentle but unshakable, as if he were reminding her they had time now. The kind of time they once thought was stolen. The kind of time that made every scar, every mistake, every lonely night feel like it had been leading here.

When he pulled back, her cheeks were flushed, her pulse thrumming in her ears.

"I don't need everything figured out," he said, his voice low, roughened by honesty. "But I want to build something real. With you. Day by day."

His words lingered in the air, more powerful than any promise. He wasn't offering perfection. He wasn't offering fairy tales. He was offering the messy, daily work of showing up.

And that, more than anything, was what she wanted.

She leaned in, kissed him again, sweet and certain. This one wasn't tentative. It wasn't twenty years of waiting. It was now. Present. Chosen.

The porch swing creaked beneath them, steady as a heartbeat, and the night wrapped around them like a blessing. Somewhere in the distance, a whippoorwill called, its song weaving through the hum of cicadas.

Rose pulled back just enough to look at him, her smile trembling but fierce.

"Acen Wheeler," she said, her voice thick with everything she hadn't dared to hope, "you're about to make this porch swing the luckiest seat in Pickwick Bend."

He laughed, soft and easy, the sound vibrating through her chest where they touched.

And somewhere between the creak of the porch swing and the call of the whippoorwill in the distance, Rose McAllister realized love wasn't about reclaiming the past.

It was about choosing the future—boldly, and with both hands.

And when Acen's hand closed over hers, strong and warm, she knew she wasn't choosing alone.

CHAPTER FORTY-THREE

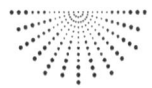

Regional finals day.

Rose took a deep breath and refused to think about pop flies and how they'd ruined it for the team last year. This was a different year. With new beginnings, and she intended to take the trophy this time.

Meanwhile, she was on the softball field with the team, tossing practice balls and trying to act normal.

"You need to swing through the pitch, Maggie, not at it like it insulted your mama's casserole," she called.

The women laughed, and for a few glorious minutes, her stress lifted like a cloud moving away from the sun. This team. These women. They would give their all to win. And that was all she needed today.

Acen was watching from the bleachers, sipping from a thermos and smiling every time Rose shouted instructions.

When practice wrapped, he walked out onto the field, brushing a strand of hair behind her ear.

"You were born to coach," he said.

"I was born to yell," she joked.

They stood there for a beat too long, the air between them charged with something tender and unfinished.

He lowered his voice. "I'm proud of you."

"Don't say that," she said, blinking fast. "You'll make me cry and ruin my tough-girl image. Today is a day to be seen as a warrior."

"I like you better when you're soft."

She laughed, but it came out wobbly.

"Don't go sweet-talking me now," she said. "We still have a game to win."

He leaned in, his voice low. "Win or lose, I've already picked my team."

The Pirate Queens' bats cracked against balls as the warm-up continued, the sharp sound echoing across the field. The morning sun was bright but not yet brutal, and the smell of freshly cut grass mingled with the tang of the chalked baselines. The dugouts hummed with chatter as the women stretched, laced cleats, and tossed balls back and forth.

Rose paced along the first-base line, eyes sharp as a hawk. Every drill mattered now. Not because it would change their muscle memory in the next hour, but because it kept their nerves from swallowing them whole.

"Ginny, keep your glove down," she barked, then softened it with a smile. "You're trying to snag butter-flies, not grounders."

Laughter rippled again, though there was tension threaded through it. Every player knew what today meant.

The Selmer Sidewinders weren't just any opponent. They were the team that had taken the trophy two years running, their pitcher known for her wicked curveball, their outfield so fast they made stealing bases look like child's play.

But this year was different. This year, the Pirate Queens weren't the underdogs. They were equals. Hungry, determined, and stitched together by more than just batting averages.

Rose tossed a ball toward Maggie again. "Drive through it. Yes! That's it." The crack of a clean hit sent the ball soaring past second base, and Maggie whooped, running halfway down the line before jogging back.

Acen's presence was steady in the bleachers, like a heartbeat she could sense even when she wasn't look-ing. He wasn't just watching the game. He was watching her. He'd made the decision not to coach with her today. This day should be hers. According to him. Instead of feeling weighed down by expectation, she felt buoyed.

The practice wound down, gloves smacking, cleats thudding against dirt, and Rose called them in. "Huddle up, ladies."

They circled close, the smell of leather, sunscreen, and determination wrapping around them like armor.

"I don't need to tell you how much this game means," Rose said. "But here's what I want you to remember. It's not about proving the town wrong. It's not about silencing whispers. It's about us. About what we've built together. Every practice, every late night, every bruise and blister. We've already won, because we did this as a team. Today is just the cherry on top."

Her voice trembled just enough to betray her heart, but no one called her on it. Instead, they stacked their hands together and shouted, "Pirate Queens!" loud enough to startle a flock of starlings from the nearby trees.

The stands were filling now, neighbors and class-mates, parents with toddlers, old timers with folding chairs dragged close to the fence. The whole town turning out. The bleachers rattled with the stomp of boots, paper programs fanned against flushed faces. Homemade posters waved in the air: *PIRATE QUEENS RULE!* and *BRING HOME THAT TROPHY!*

"Listen up, y'all," Rose said, hands on her hips. "The Sidewinders think they've got us beat. They're taller, they're younger, they've got more travel-ball experi-ence. But none of them knows what it means to wear

Pirate red. We fight for each other. Every inning, every pitch, every play. That's how we win."

The women stomped and cheered, fists pounding the air. The sound rolled across the field like thunder.

The hum of chatter in the stands grew into a roar as the announcer's voice crackled through the loudspeaker, calling both teams to the dugouts.

The Selmer Sidewinders strutted onto the field in crisp green uniforms, smirks flashing as they stretched. The Pirate Queens answered with steady steps, red jerseys gleaming under the sun, their logo, a heart-shaped softball with the team name embroidered on it, bold across their chests.

Rose's throat tightened. This was it.

The first inning was all nerves.

The ump's call echoed: *"Play ball!"*

The first pitch cracked against the catcher's mitt. The crowd roared.

The Sidewinders came out swinging, their leadoff batter slamming a double down the third-base line. The crowd roared, half in triumph, half in worry. Rose's chest tightened, but she clapped her hands, calling, "Shake it off! Next one, let's go!"

The Pirate Queens' pitcher, Tasha, took a breath, rolled her shoulders, and delivered three blazing strikes to the next batter. The crowd erupted in cheers, stomping the bleachers so hard the metal rang.

By the time the third out came, the Sidewinders had managed one run. Not great, but not insurmountable.

"Okay, ladies," Rose said, as her team grabbed bats. "Let's answer back."

Maggie stepped up to the plate, adjusting her helmet, chin high. The Sidewinders' pitcher smirked, wound up, and let loose that infamous curveball. Maggie swung. And missed. The crowd groaned.

But Rose clapped. "You saw it! Now you know. Reset!"

Second pitch. Crack. The ball sailed over the short-stop's head, dropping into the grass for a clean single. The Pirate Queens' dugout exploded in cheers.

By the time the inning ended, both teams had scored once.

The game stretched into a battle of wills. Inning after inning, bats cracked, gloves snapped, dirt flew. The crowd grew louder with every play, children chanting, adults hollering, the old timers slapping knees and muttering about the glory days.

Rose shouted herself hoarse, pacing the dugout, clapping until her palms stung. She wasn't just coaching. She was willing every ball, every step, every swing to go their way.

Acen's gaze was steady from the stands, and sometimes, when the tension coiled too tight, she'd glance at him. He'd tip his thermos, nodding as if to say, *You've got this.*

By the top of the seventh, the score was tied 4–4.

The trophy sat gleaming on a table near the announcer's booth, sunlight catching on its polished surface.

So close, and yet it felt miles away.

The Sidewinders were up to bat, and their slugger sent a screaming line drive toward center field. For a heartbeat, the crowd gasped. But Dani sprinted, glove outstretched, and snagged it mid-air, tumbling into the grass. She popped up, ball in hand, triumphant.

The Pirate Queens roared, slapping the dugout rail, screaming themselves breathless. Rose's heart pounded so hard she thought it might bruise her ribs.

Two outs later, they jogged in, bats ready.

"This is it," Rose told them, voice shaking with adrenaline. "Bottom of the seventh. Our house. Our time."

Maggie got on base with a sharp single. The next batter bunted, moving her to second. The tension was unbearable—one run could end it.

Then came Dani. Her helmet tilted forward, eyes narrowed. She swung hard on the second pitch.

Crack.

The ball soared high, arcing toward left field. The crowd rose to its feet, a single collective breath held tight. The Sidewinder outfielder sprinted back, back— then stumbled. The ball dropped just past her glove, rolling to the fence.

Maggie tore around third, cleats kicking up dust. Rose screamed herself hoarse, waving her in.

The throw came late. Maggie slid across home plate, arms outstretched, and the umpire bellowed, "Safe!"

The stadium erupted. Fans poured from the bleachers, voices merging into a tidal wave of sound. The Pirate Queens leapt from the dugout, gloves tossed, arms flung around each other as they screamed and danced.

Rose stood frozen, tears blurring her eyes as the reality hit. They'd done it. They'd finally done it.

Acen was suddenly beside her, wrapping his arms around her waist and lifting her off the ground. "You did it, Coach," he whispered, voice rough with pride.

"*We* did it," she corrected, laughing through tears. "All of us."

The trophy was carried to the field, shining under the setting sun. The women passed it hand to hand, kissing it, lifting it high as the crowd chanted, "Pirate Queens! Pirate Queens!"

Rose touched the cool metal, her heart thundering. Not just from the win, but from everything it meant. Redemption. Belonging. A future she could finally believe in.

Acen pressed his forehead to hers as fireworks cracked in the distance, some enthusiastic fan having set them off early.

"This is just the beginning," he murmured.

And Rose, standing on the dirt with her team screaming around her and the trophy in her hands, believed him.

EPILOGUE

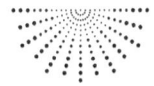

T *Two months later*

The leaves had turned gold and copper, and Rose could already smell apple butter and firewood in the air. Autumn had settled into Pickwick Bend like a favorite sweater—warm, a little worn in, and exactly right.

The moon hung low over the lake as Rose and Acen sat side-by-side on the porch swing.

"I've been thinking," he said, nudging her shoulder. "We should have a fall softball scrimmage. Co-ed. Costumes optional."

Rose laughed. "Only if Cindy agrees to dress as a catcher again. That chest guard changed her personality."

Acen chuckled, then grew quiet.

"I've also been thinking about something else," he added, reaching into his jacket pocket.

Her heart skipped. "You're not pulling out jewelry, are you?"

"Nope." He held up a folded piece of paper.

She opened it. It was a lease.

For a little blue house on Elderberry Lane.

"You want to move in together?" she asked, heart thudding.

"I do," he said. "Eventually, maybe we'll build something bigger. But for now, I want you and me under one roof. Shared coffee mugs. Morning walks. Pillow-stealing arguments. All of it." He looked around the porch where they sat and smiled. "I know this is where you grew up. That your parents left it to you. But maybe we could start fresh in a place we create together."

Rose hesitated. He was right about her feelings for this place. They ran bone deep. But maybe Acen was right. Maybe they needed a place with no ghosts.

"Riley would love to take over this place. I think he was a bit jealous when Mama and Daddy left it to me. But he was living in Knoxville back then and didn't need a place here like I did."

As soon as the words left her mouth, she knew it was the right thing to do. Riley could sell his new build house that he'd bought when he moved back to Pickwick Bend and take over their family home. Who knew? Maybe Riley would find someone to share his life and make it into a family home again.

She smiled at Acen and rattle the paper in her hand. "So… we sign this?"

"Only if you want to."

Rose leaned in, kissed him soft and slow.

"I want to."

He tucked the paper back in his jacket, and they settled into the swing, the world quiet around them.

And somewhere between the rustle of wind in the trees and the warmth of their joined hands, Rose realized:

This was the kind of story she never thought she'd get.

And she'd written every page herself.

THANK YOU FOR READING *Curve Balls and Second Chances*.

SNEAK PEEK BOOK 2

Keeping reading for a sneak peek at Book 2

In the *Pickwick Pirate Queens Softball Romance Books* *Curveballs and Commitments*

Curve Balls and Commitments

Tasha Carter is the spitfire of Pickwick Bend's women's softball team—a walk-up playlist queen, ace pitcher, and undefeated in every dance battle. But when her plans to launch a dance fitness studio get delayed, and two very different men start vying for her attention, Tasha finds herself juggling more than just batting practice.

One is sweet, steady, and already part of the team's inner circle. The other is a smooth-talking big-city transplant with charm, ambition, and a mysterious past.

Tasha has always played hard and loved harder. But

when the bases are loaded and her heart's on the line, will she choose the teammate who's been there all along, or the stranger who makes her feel seen in a brand-new way?